THE TOE

AND OTHER TALES

THE TOE

AND OTHER TALES BY
ALEXANDER HARVEY

Short Story Index Reprint Series

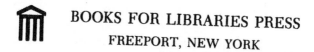

BOOKS FOR LIBRARIES PRESS
FREEPORT, NEW YORK

First Published 1913
Reprinted 1970

STANDARD BOOK NUMBER:
8369-3582-9

LIBRARY OF CONGRESS CATALOG CARD NUMBER:
73-125215

PRINTED IN THE UNITED STATES OF AMERICA

To
Edward
Jewitt
Wheeler.

CONTENTS

THE TOE

AS she dressed with punctilious care before the cheval glass in her bed-room,
it amazed Helen that she, a wife, could
prepare for a guilty hour with a lover in so
matter-of-fact a mood. Sin, she reflected,
drawing the sheer silk of her open-work blue
stockings across her cheek, must be like
everything else in life. To be false to her
marriage vows—how tremendous and melo-
dramatic such a thing had appeared but a
few weeks back! That was before Jack
Marmaduke had forced her lips against his
own while with flashing eyes she cried:
"Sir!"

No doubt her husband would kill Jack
if ever exposure came. Even that prospect
did not seem shocking to Helen. She was
astonished to find how interested she had be-

come in the hand embroidery of her chemise, lying daintily on the bed. She tried hard to think of monogamy as the basis of Western civilization, only to have her vagrant mind wander back to her own rounded bust reflected so tenderly in the glass before her.

But time was pressing. Her rendezvous with Jack was for three o'clock that very afternoon. The miniature golden timepiece on her dressing-table chimed the approach of that guilty hour. What a wealth of underwear was sprawled over the bed in masses of lace edging, soft-finish nainsook and French lawn! Jack, she knew instinctively, was a Sybarite, an adept in the technic of sin. She had read a popular novel once about a wicked but fascinating Justice of the United States Supreme Court whose delight it was to kiss his mistresses between the shoulder blades. Jack would, no doubt, kiss her between the shoulder blades—a thing her husband, the famous biologist, never did. Well, she would deck herself for this sin as if it were a consecration in lingerie. And was it sin, after all? Was not the old ethic exploded in this age of radium emanations and wireless telegraphy? The fine nainsook on her bed, with its wealth of Valenciennes lace, of sheer lawn, of white silk ribbons, seemed to cry aloud that her affair with Jack would have its beauty. Never could she prepare to meet her husband, upon his return from a lecture tour through the West, in this æsthetic way. That dainty and fussy silk petticoat, with its deep flounces and its inserted gores of plaited silk —what an ecstasy it promised! Oh, she would be a dainty thing to step into a paramour's arms. And she, a Puritan in every fibre, as she supposed, was not shocked. That seemed very odd. Perhaps, after all, sin was not the thing of sex she had been trained from girlhood to surmise.

This tremendous event had come into Helen's life at a time when American women were wearing very little in the way

of underwear and reading a great deal in
the way of Ibsen. Her lingerie and her
literature were of the thinnest and lightest. Helen's husband stinted her in nothing. Her surplice corset cover was developed through exquisite flouncing. With it
that afternoon she would wear a five-gored
petticoat in round length so that when she
stepped out of the tailored directoire gown
her attitude might be sacerdotal in its dignity. Her meeting with Jack was to be
no less sacred than the frenzy of a Delphic
priestess. Helen had taken no risks with
the corset cover. It had soft, indefinite, lacy
effects. Two rows of edging, joined with
beading, formed the shoulder straps. Helen
was cunning enough to realize that one cannot get a well-fitting corset cover by gathering in the entire fullness at the back and
in the front. Her device was to slant it
at the under-arm as if it were a waist. This
made the garment conform to the lines of
her figure, which she well knew had inspired

in Jack the longing of Tereus for Procne. She understood how to dress as thoroughly as Napoleon understood how to outflank Mack at Ulm.

Helen strove to fix her thoughts upon Voltaire's views of God as she took the lattice ribbon corset from its repose upon her bed, scanning it critically. Is the human mind duplex, she asked herself, and can a beautiful wife contemplate a pair of stays made expressly for her own slender figure —lighter in weight than anything of the sort in a varied experience of these cunningly boned creations—while meditating upon her own cosmopolitan soul? It must be so. Helen wondered at the tendency of her mind, while pondering the circumstance that a corset should be unlaced to its fullest extent before being put on, to take refuge in enthusiasm for Rousseau against the thought of her husband. She was trying to be shocked and was failing. She sighed as she hooked the corset at the bottom first and then hooked the top. Having hooked the top, she undid the bottom and hooked the corset all the way down, resolving as she did so to read Nietzsche every night of the sinful life she was beginning. How childish her delight, she reflected, in the thing of white silk now shaping itself in pink ribbon daintiness about her waist line. To think that a waist line had had more to do with the course of human history under the Roman Emperors than even economic determinism! She resolved to discuss that theme with the brilliant young Socialist who sneered at marriage so poetically and whom she had encountered at a woman suffragist debate a few weeks ago. Did he, too, kiss women between the shoulder blades in these revolutionary times?

She stood erect before the mirror that she might be more at ease in adjusting the corset well down, with lacings loose, while she worked her trim figure up until it fitted in well over the hips. At last she began her snug lacing at the waist line and then laced above and below, not without a fleeting thought of the proletariat in Odessa, for Helen was above all else a woman of comprehensive sympathies—what is known nowadays as an intellectual.

At no stage of these proceedings did she lose her odd sense of not being shocked at all. She was not overwhelmed by any consciousness of sin. She did not even think of Jack, not even of her husband. She was thinking only of a low bust, of a flat back, of small hips, as the essentials of womanhood. Sex is in these things. Did her husband, in his learned monographs on the behavior of the lower organisms, ever pause to ask how the forces of sex in the primitive protoplasm of unicellular creatures had evolved a tailored waist, round and slightly accentuated at the hips, with a straight, flat, unbroken line down the front of a paneled skirt? What biological principle could be behind the circumstance that for a woman with a well-developed figure a plain, tight-fitting corset cover is the most useful thing on earth? Did Madame Roland, Helen asked herself, think of her bust when she stood beneath that statue of Liberty and uttered that immortal apostrophe? That agonizing but suave curve from the shoulder to the top of the bust of Madame Roland—what could it mean but a good corset? Nay, was not the cause of woman in the wonderful twentieth century bound up in some subtle way with that lovely, straight line from the chin to the knees which made the ladies' tailors allies, without realizing it, in a great struggle between the sexes? Had Mary Wollstonecraft, with all her genius, achieved as much for woman as one well-made corset?

How time was flying! She was to meet Jack at a station of the subway far up town. She walked as far as Forty-second street, feeling, she said to herself reproachfully, far prouder of those suave curves at her hip

and shoulder than she ever could of the intimacy she had gained with Nietzsche. Helen
wondered, as she bought her ticket at the
little booth, whether the Superwoman would
be long-waisted. It was fully ten minutes
to three by the time Helen had arrived at
that station of the subway from which she
and her lover were to proceed to the scene
of their sin. Jack was nowhere in sight.
She had made him promise to get to the
uptown station precisely at three, not a
minute before. She did not want to alight
from a train in the subway only to be
accosted by a man who had obviously been
awaiting her.

A feeling of annoyance brought a flush to
Helen's cheek as she realized how precipitate she had been. It was quite impossible
for a woman of Helen's inexpressibly elegant appearance to linger ten minutes in a
subway station. There was no alternative
but to make her way above to the street.
There she might find some tea-room or de-

partment store to kill the hateful minutes in. She emerged into the sunlight and made for the first soda water fountain that offered itself.

Eight minutes to three! The soda water fountain was besieged by impatient throngs of that class of women who have never heard of a Nietzsche, never read an Ibsen. What was biology to that fat woman pouring liquid chocolate into her frightful gullet? Helen sighed as she bought a ten-cent ticket from the cashier and seated herself upon a hard, high stool. She kicked her well-shod and tiny foot against the counter in sheer vexation. She turned cold with horror the next moment, for the impatient movement had forced her toe right through the silken texture of her stocking. This was an accident to which Helen was peculiarly liable. It was her habit to wear open-work silk stockings just a size too small for her feet. She loved the feeling of pressure that went with silk stretched to the utmost and she

way as she could. She did not dare look
towards the kiosk that led below the street
level, lest Jack's form should loom there.
Her social peril, the narrow escape she had
had from the most compromising possibility a civilized woman can face, and ever
so many considerations allied to these filled
her brain as she hailed a taxicab and was
whirled back to her husband's home. Never,
she told herself, could she seize again that
first fine careless rapture at the thought of
ascertaining just what life, real life, was
like. The double standard of morals, the
possibility of enlarging the narrowness of
woman's existence by tasting the flavor of
man's experience, would be associated in her
mind hereafter, not with George Sand and
Mary Wollstonecraft, but with a hole in
her stocking. The subject had been hurled
over the line that sunders sublimity from
the absurd. Had her husband seen that toe
protruding through the hole in her stocking,
the episode would have been delightful. They

would have had a merry laugh over it together.

As the taxicab halted before her husband's door, the significance of the adventure she had just lived through flashed upon Helen's more composed mind. She had run against the bulwarks of monogamy when she thrust her toe through her stocking. A woman could confront her husband without loss of prestige or of her moral ascendancy after such an accident. But she could not face a lover with dignity.

The psychology of this, Helen felt, was subtle. The things that tell against monogamy are great things, to be sure—the hunger of the heart for perfect love, the soul that finds itself understood when the ideal mate arrives at last, the supremely human impulse, and the revolt of the intellect against the slavery of tradition.

These, and things like these, tell against monogamy.

Working for it are the little things—the

feeling of ease in one's world, the need of a life in harmony with that of narrow minds, the conventions, the financial obligations and even the holes that are worn in one's stockings. There are, after all, but a few great things. There are, after all, so many little things. And this world is made for the little things, the little minds, the little lives, the little spirits, the little matings. Ah! the wonder is not that monogamy survives but that anyone can resist it and survive. The things making for monogamy belong to what Bismarck called the imponderabilia, but their influence must have been immense during that long, prehistoric period in which man was toiling up the slope that led from life in tree-tops to a civilization that encased the feminine limb in stockings of the sheerest silk. Not that primitive women thrust their toes through stockings and thus arrived at monogamy. There was in their time some other force or circumstance working for monogamy. But whatever it was, Helen reflected, as she paid for the taxicab, it induced in the female of our species the feeling that whatever happened a wife must be true to her husband. Helen let herself in at the front door with a profound reverence for the seventh commandment.

THE RAFT

"DON'T kill one of the others," he said. "Kill me. I am not so starved as they."

"Griggs," I replied, "has begged me to kill him first."

The emaciated passenger turned as I said the words and shot a look at Griggs. The twelve days we had spent on that raft in the trackless ocean had set the seal of starvation upon each of us, although the young woman bore it best, but Griggs had suffered unspeakably.

He was prostrate against the solitary water barrel which a rain had filled the night before. But for that Griggs must have died, surely. The girl was holding the wet end of a rag to his lips.

"I suppose," I said, slowly, and with

pain, for the long-drawn-out agony of thirst and starvation seemed to have affected my throat most of all, "I suppose there's no use hoping for land or a sail."

Before the starving man could reply, the girl had made her way to where we crouched. The sea was running high, but she did not crawl when she moved about, as did the rest of us.

"I know what you men have been talking about these two days," she said.

There she paused. So weak was this young creature from lack of food and drink that her voice was the merest whisper. I wanted to support her with an arm, but my weakness had grown upon me since the last biscuit was eaten, and I could do no more than get up on my hands and knees. I felt dizzy.

"Can we not," she said, "wait another day before anyone is killed and eaten?"

"You've made us wait two days as it is," I managed to answer. "Another twenty-four hours of this and there won't be any of us alive to eat at all. That's why I want to be killed and eaten here and now."

I sank back to the board that had been my bed for so many hungry hours. I had not spoken so much for a week. The effort tried me like felling timber.

The girl placed her skinny elbow beneath my head and placed her lips against my ear.

"I've saved a mouthful of bread for you," she whispered.

The next moment there was a running stream down the inside of my cheeks, like a flood. The feeling had been brought on by the bit of food the girl had put stealthily on the end of my tongue. I nearly gasped as I moved that bite of crust into the side of my jaw where my teeth came down upon it like sledge hammers. I chewed furtively two or three times, for I was afraid to let them see me do it. Not that they would have fallen upon me. They were all too weak. But I knew that the sight of me eating a lump of bread would prove to my companions on that raft as tormenting as fire and faggot.

The girl had left my side and was now standing beside the Dutch cook. I could not see his face, but the sight of her lips close to the big, hairy ear gave me an idea.

"Jinks!" I whispered as loudly as I could.

The emaciated passenger who had begged me to kill him turned his gaunt eyes upon me when he heard his name.

"That girl gave you a mouthful of bread yesterday when she whispered in your ear."

He bent his head.

"She's just given me a mouthful of bread. I believe she's giving the cook a mouthful now."

We both looked over towards the sea chest against which the cook's head was propped. The girl had crossed the raft to where the improvised mast bore its fluttering signal of distress, but the cook was furtively chewing a mouthful.

I crawled upon my hands and knees to where the girl was.

"I'll kill the next man you feed," I said. "Eat your bread yourself."

"You got the last mouthful," she said.

Never a suspicion that she might be lying crossed my mind. I paid no more attention to the girl. My mind was obsessed by another notion. I thought I would swoon as I retraced my path to where Jinks was lying.

"Say!" I said, hoarsely, "you say you're willing to die to make a meal for the rest of us?"

"My God, yes!"

"How are we going to kill you?"

Jinks stared wildly about. There were two blunt knives aboard and an axe. I took no stock in the axe. Not one of us had the strength left to lift it. The knives were too blunt to be of use in opening a vein, for the simple reason that every man on the raft had been brought so low by hunger and weakness that he could not have pressed it even against his own skinny wrist.

"I'll tie a handkerchief about my throat and strangle," said Jinks.

He had the knot tied in a jiffy, but he was too weak to pull with enough energy for strangulation. He gave up in five minutes and lay still.

But the procedure of Jinks had given me a suggestion. I crawled over to the one bit of rope still with us. It bound the timbers of the raft we had hastily constructed when the ship went down. But try as I might, it was too strongly knotted to be unloosed by any effort of a starving man.

Here was a crisis, indeed. Our one hope of life was the slaughter of a man, but here were we too weak from loss of food and drink to be capable of murder.

"Mr. Blake!"

Starved though I was, I almost started

up. The girl's lips were once more at my ear.

"I must tell you something," she gasped.

Her long hair fell in a cascade about my face. She turned to look at the others behind me, as if she were fearful of some secret of which she might be sole guardian. In another moment I knew what the secret was, because she bent her head over mine and kissed my lips.

How cool her mouth was! It was like a long, cold drink.

"Now you know," she whispered. "I love you. Wait one more day for me."

In another minute she was making her way back to the cook's side. I saw her dip her rag into the flowing sea and swab his horrible feet as he lay against the sea chest. But I thought no more of death.

Slowly and heavily the burning sun dropped into the waters far beyond the sky. Out peered the stars. The starving men all about me lay like logs of the raft that bore them on, on. I could barely discern the shadows we made as midnight drew forward and brought the moon up the sky.

"Blake!"

I turned my head slowly at this whisper of my name. It was Griggs.

"Let us hang on another day," he whispered. Then he swooned.

"Yes," I whispered, in an hour, when he recovered consciousness. "Let us hang on."

I no longer remembered, as I said the words, that our last bite of food had gone down our throats the day before; that our last few pints of water were in the barrel beneath the mast. I would live for love. Griggs crawled back to where the cook lay.

"My darling!"

I barely caught the whisper, but I had seen her coming and the sight revived me. I tried to put an arm about her waist, but only a hand reached hers.

"Dearest," she whispered, "don't let them see us."

She had kissed my lips and gone before I could utter a word. It was as well, for in a moment more I was looking into the glaring eyes of Jinks.

"We'll wait another day," he said; "another day before I die to feed you all."

His face was withdrawn, but I had not the strength to gaze after his retreating figure. Nor did I think of death any more. My mind ran on that devoted girl. How pretty she seemed among the starving thirty of us! Would she come back and kiss me once again? I managed to lift my head from the bottom of the raft and turned it for a sight of her. The blackness of a Pacific night was upon the deep, yet I could see the outline of the sea chest, behind which she retreated for sleep when the shadows fell. The cook's bulk obscured its outline to my glance, for he was sprawled in front of it. The dawn could not be far away, unless the stars were lying, but the sea was rising and falling heavily like a sleeper in pain. A vague alarm for her seized me on a sudden, and I essayed to walk to where she was.

I could not get upon my feet. Upon my hands and knees I moved like a shadow. Had I the wealth of Ormuzd and of Ind I would have given all of it to be able to speak her name aloud. But what was her name? It dawned upon me for the first time since we kissed that I knew not her name nor anything about her. She was one of the passengers in the wrecked ship. So was I. Then she could not possibly know my full name, unless some purser or steward had revealed it. Well, I would question her regarding these things when I had reached her side.

Would I ever do so? Minute after minute I spent crawling to the chest. The starving men lay in slumber or in swoon, quite motionless. I wondered if the cook, too, could be asleep.

My head swam from the exertion of so much of my strength as was left after these long days without food or drink. I collapsed and lay motionless, until repose should have brought back some capacity to use my knees and hands.

I heard whispers. Her voice! Slowly I wrenched my neck about until my eyes were on a level with the top of the sea chest. There I clung, fearing the swoon.

"Darling!"

"Wait one day for the woman who loves you."

Then I heard the sound of a kiss.

Slowly and silently I dragged myself to the top of the sea chest. A strange fury had brought me strength. I peered down upon the girl.

She had one arm about the cook's neck. Her long hair swept his face. I could see by the light of the moon that his horrible paw rested upon her shoulder. I would have given this world for strength enough to clutch her by the throat.

"Wait one more day for me, beloved!" I

heard her whisper. Then she stole around to the other side of the chest.

I was waiting for her. Resisting an impulse to drag her with me into that running sea—an impulse for which rage and hate would have given me strength—I hissed:

"Wanton! I saw you kiss that Dutch fiend. I heard every word you spoke to him!"

The little blood left in me rushed to my brain and I fell beside the chest. She crawled to where I lay and put an arm about me.

I bit her.

"Leave me!" I managed to groan faintly. "Leave me!"

I could just make out the dawn at the other extremity of the horizon. I resolved that this day would bring my death.

"I had to do it," I heard her whisper, as she placed her lips to my ear. "That Dutchman would have killed one of you a week ago for food, but I made love to him to save our lives. I took his knife away while he had still strength left to use it and I threw it into the sea."

"You lie!" I managed to hiss out. "Griggs wanted to die that we might eat him."

"Yes, and I won him over to life with my kisses."

"Vile woman!"

I wanted to roar the words, but my voice scarcely attained the volume of a whisper. She had placed my head in her lap and I lay looking up helplessly into her face. Fury filled me and I tried to call for help.

"Jinks!" I moaned. "Jinks!"

"Jinks will do nothing for you," she whispered. "I have bought him, too with my kisses. I have bribed every man on this raft to wait by telling him he alone has my love."

She relaxed her hold of my neck and leaned against the chest like a woman in a faint. I watched her closed eyes with the helpless fury of a starving man.

"Had I the strength," I muttered, "I

would throw you into these waters. You have been the ruin of us all."

"I have saved you," she whispered. "Look!"

I followed her pointing finger with my eye, and upon the waters, lit up now by the dawn, I saw a sail.

THE FOOLS

AS he reposed in the satin-lined coffin, with a wreath of roses at his head and his hands folded across his breast, Cornelius Heston observed carefully every detail of the preparations going on about him for his own funeral. This was the second day of the trance in which, from the first moment of it, he had seemed to himself like a man turned into marble. When they dressed him for the grave he passed into an insensibility so complete that no knowedge of the circumstances attending his conveyance from the bed, in which the physician had pronounced him dead, to the library, in which he lay in state, could add a detail to what he now remembered. Through the lashes which nearly veiled his eyes he discerned a row of books against an opposite

38

wall. He saw the carved oak door of the library. The servant had left the room not half an hour ago, remarking to the butler that the undertaker's men would arrive shortly to convey the body to the vault. The door had closed behind the pair with no suspicion in their minds that the man in his coffin had been making desperate efforts to move a hand or wink an eye—in vain.

A bronze clock on the mantel chimed the hour of seven as Heston lay immovable in the luxury of the casket. He wondered whether it could be seven in the morning or seven in the evening. His conjectures were interrupted by the opening of the library door. He saw his wife steal slowly into the room. From head to foot, Mrs. Heston was arrayed in black. Even in that grim hour, he could notice how superbly the beauty of her figure revealed itself against the riot of color formed by the volumes on the shelves. The woman advanced to the coffin

until Heston actually met the look in her
eyes. Eva's countenance wore the cold com-
posure habitual to her. Her masses of hair
were coiled in the fashion suggested by the
young artist who had painted her portrait
for the woman suffragists. Mrs. Heston
owed some measure of her fame to the beauty
she had inherited from a French ancestress,
but she was indebted for her national ce-
lebrity to the eloquence she had exploited in
vindicating the right of her sex to the bal-
lot. For the first time since this trance left
him rigid, it occurred to Heston that his wife
had, after all, no real need of him. She would
find in her labors for humanity refuge from
the grief of his going. Perhaps that idea
had been latent in his mind when first he
realized his plight.

Mrs. Heston placed one of her perfect
hands upon the brow of her husband. Next
she lifted the wreath from his head and
tossed it to the floor. Finally she walked to
the foot of the coffin and drummed absent-

mindedly upon the edge of it with her fingers. Heston could see every feature of her
face. She was looking at herself in the mirror over the mantelpiece. Heston inferred
this from the coquettish expression about
which he had often teased her. There was
a rose in her hand. Mrs. Heston arranged
it carefully in her hair as she hummed an
aria from Bizet's masterpiece.

Then she practiced a two-step.

The man in the coffin became suddenly
conscious of a burning sensation at the tip
of one of his fingers. Yet he was helpless
still. A step sounded outside. Once more
the library door opened—this time to admit
a man.

"Jack!" cried Mrs. Heston.

The newcomer took the woman in his
arms. Heston looked on while his wife laid
her head upon her lover's shoulder. He rec-
ognized this man too well. He was the brilliant John Calvin Idell, champion in the
press and on the platform of that crusade in

behalf of woman which is yet to create a new heaven and a new earth.

"Dearest!" she cried softly, allowing her lover to lay a hat and an overcoat upon the coffin. "What kept you so long?"

"I was in Chicago when your telegram reached me," replied the suffragist agitator.

His arm was around her waist. Side by side they gazed at Heston's cold face.

"Well," remarked Idell, after a silent pause, "he's gone."

"Yes, darling," she murmured softly. "I'm free."

They exchanged a kiss.

"What killed him?"

"Heart disease, the doctor said."

Idell took his gaze from the face in the coffin.

"When's the funeral?"

"I'll just have it taken to the vault," she remarked, as her head sank once more upon the lover's shoulder. "There are to be some prayers here in the morning."

"I stopped at the undertaker's on my way," Idell said. "His men will be here at eight."

"Then let's go upstairs," she suggested. "You can come down to see them."

They stood locked in each other's arms for a moment more.

"Who would have expected this," said Idell, "during that happy week in Philadelphia last spring?"

Heston remembered that week. His wife had been a heroine of the woman suffrage convention in the Quaker City. Idell had made the speech of the occasion.

"Shall I ever forget that week in Philadelphia!" the man in the coffin heard his wife murmur. "The first time you ever kissed me was when I asked you to prepare my lecture on Mary Wollstonecraft."

They were beside the coffin once more and Heston saw them kiss.

"Come," said Idell, taking his hat and overcoat from the coffin and throwing them upon a sofa. "I'll take you upstairs. Those undertakers may be here any minute."

Heston heard the library door close behind the paramours. He scarcely heeded the sound. The shock of what he had just lived through was bringing him back to life. The burning in his finger tip had been succeeded by a burning in his feet. He was winking his eyelids. He could detect the beating of his own heart.

Suddenly, he sat upright in the coffin. They had prepared him for burial in a shroud, he noticed now. Trembling in every limb, he thrust one foot over the edge of the casket. There was a lighted taper at the head of the bier and a fire in the library grate. He got out of the coffin, as he remembered getting out of a skiff, without toppling it from its supports. He stood giddily upon his feet, mechanically rubbing his limbs. Life was warming him. So much he realized with a strange sense of power over the people who had just quitted the room. In another moment he was crouching beside the fire, a hand at his chin. In five minutes more he withdrew to his coffin and resumed his pacific posture, folding his hands again across his breast.

He had not long to wait. He heard the step of Idell upon the stairs. Mrs. Heston's paramour entered the library and closed the door behind him. Heston could move his eyes freely by this time. He kept them fixed upon Idell, who seated himself upon a sofa and drew a wallet from an inner pocket of his coat. Heston saw Idell count the money. He even discerned the denomination of the bills. The paramour pocketed his wallet and sauntered over to the coffin.

"Fool!" murmured Idell. "Damned fool!"

Those were his last words. Heston sat bolt upright in the coffin and clutched Idell by the throat. The husband was soon atop of the paramour on the carpeted floor, stifling every sound in a grip that never relaxed.

One minute, two minutes, three minutes passed silently. Heston's roving eye caught sight of his wife's hat at the foot of the sofa. He drew it to him with a foot. Extracting the hat-pin with a grimness of fury that seemed to him then and ever afterwards like sheer insanity, Heston drove it deep into the base of Idell's skull. The paramour lay dead on the floor.

"Fool!" muttered Heston, standing in his shroud over the body of his victim. "Damned fool!"

In a trice he was stripping the corpse. One by one, Heston donned the articles of the dead man's attire, a task of some difficulty, for the pair were not of the same height and girth. When at last he stood arrayed in Idell's clothes, even to the hat and overcoat, Heston put the shroud upon the corpse and laid it in the coffin. Idell looked strangely cold and dignified in death. Resisting an impulse to summon his wife to the library, Heston took up the dead man's cane and made for the door. He had clothes and money and a brother in Central America. From that night he would be a different man in another world.

There was a ring at the front door. Heston thrust Idell's hat well down over his brow and wrapped the lapels of Idell's overcoat about his chin. There was a step outside. He heard the butler tell the men to go into the library. Heston himself opened the door for them. He closed it swiftly when the visitors came in. The butler retreated to the kitchen.

"I suppose you're the undertaker's men," Heston said in a whisper.

"Yes, sir," was the whispered reply. "We've brought the embalming fluid."

"None of that," whispered Heston again. "Mrs. Heston told me to say she can't hear of such a thing. Suppose her husband were alive?"

With these words he lifted the lid of the coffin and placed it over the corpse. The men produced their screw-drivers. Their task occupied them a full five minutes, at the end of which Heston took out Idell's wallet and gave the pair a dollar each. They went away gratefully. Standing on the front steps the husband watched the receding shadows of the undertaker's men until a youthful figure halted at the door. It was the newsboy, delivering the evening paper. Mechanically, Heston received it and, for the sake of saving appearances, unfolded the sheet. The first thing to meet his eyes was a reproduction of his wife's face in coarse half-tone. She had been interviewed that very morning, apparently, by a clever lady journalist, to whom Mrs. Heston confided her well-known view that the nineteenth century having been that of Marriage, the twentieth would be that of Love.

"Fool!" muttered Heston as he crumpled the paper in his hand and strode to the railroad station. "Damned fool!"

THE FINISHING TOUCH

THERE they lay, like so many death warrants, the letters that proved up to the hilt the infidelity of his wife to her marriage vows.

Philander Watts had come upon these damning epistles by the merest accident. His romantic and shapely wife had betaken herself that morning to the home of her mother. Philander himself, impelled by a sudden summons to the West in the negotiation of one of his many real estate operations, bethought him of a small valise he had seen in his wife's hand upon her return from a recent sojourn at Palm Beach. A preliminary search of her scented bedroom failed to disclose the thing. By mere chance, Philander raised the lid of a carved oak desk.

There lay the black bag.

49

The young husband found the article locked. Why he made an instant search for the key, finding it at last in a tiny pigeonhole of the dainty desk, he could not have explained, even to himself. When the valise was unlocked it contained only a withered rose.

That at any rate was the first hasty impression of Philander. Not until he had returned to his own bedroom and was putting some articles of apparel into the bag did one of its inner pockets bulge open to reveal the guilty letters.

There were but three of these. Each was more damning than the spot of blood against which Lady Macbeth ranted. All were signed with the name of Angus. The stationery was that of the hotel at Palm Beach from which Philander's wife had returned, with her maid and her babe, some five weeks before. The progress of an amour was recorded in the correspondence with an art as sublime as it was unconscious. Of burning

kisses exchanged in the darkness of starry
midnight, of limbs entwined, of the sated vo-
racity of love reposing with exhausted sighs
—of these and things akin to these the letters told poetically. Through the medium
of three guilty letters Philander could ex-
plore whole continents of a world of woman
he had never glimpsed before.

Sinking upon his bed with a gasp as he
finished the last of these too human documents, the eye of Philander was lured instinctively to that miraculously appetizing
portrait of his wife which reflected such glory
upon the genius of the painter, Robert
Henri. The great artist had brought the
beauty of Philander's wife out of that canvas
with all the divine power of a Jove evoking
Minerva from his own head. The intoxicating slope of the bared arm, the delicate droop
of the head, the maddening line of the bust
were subtly blended in the portrait at which
Philander now gazed in the mood of Prome-
theus contemplating the vulture that de-

voured him. In a sudden access of fury he sprang to his feet and shook a clenched fist at the painted face looking so wistfully from the wall upon his soul's crucifixion. He even rushed forward with some frenzied thought of tearing the masterpiece from its frame. He had once lifted his hand against the radiant original.

That was before their marriage. The woman who was now his wife had long dallied with his pleadings. Marriage, the fair Eudora had insisted again and again, was not her vocation. She must live for Art. Yet would she not let Philander go. For weeks she had maddened him thus. At last, beside himself one evening when her refusal of his suit had taken a wickedly mocking form, Philander had seized Eudora and reversing her upon his knee literally—there is no other word for it—spanked the temperamental thing. The task concluded, Philander collapsed. Eudora, who had submitted in utter silence, was the first to speak.

"Philander," she said meekly, "I will marry you."

Neither had referred ever again to the episode. But it occurred to Philander now in his agony. It was borne in upon him that he could not gaze upon the face of his wife without striking her. He dare not let her divine from his agitation that he had penetrated her guilty secret. He must lose no time in regaining his freedom from this creature of beauty and of lust. The letters of Angus must be traced to their author.

Who was he?

The handwriting was quite unfamiliar to Philander. The guilty correspondence was evidently carried on in the Palm Beach hotel at which Eudora had spent a period of recuperation the previous winter. Thither, Philander felt, he must now repair.

There was a giddiness in the head of the young husband as he picked up the valise and walked unsteadily back to his wife's apartment. He shivered as he restored the fatal piece of baggage to the desk. He turned to leave a boudoir heavy with a perfume that sickened him now when the tiny key he had abstracted from its pigeonhole recurred to his memory. In a trice, that, too, was restored.

It was now well on in the afternoon. He must catch a train for Palm Beach without delay. Hurrying to his study, Philander dashed off a note apprising Eudora that business had summoned him West for a week. There was nothing in such a circumstance to seem unusual. Eudora herself was prone to sudden journeys in quest of that recuperation which the temperamental crises of her being rendered indispensable.

In forty-eight hours Philander Watts was registered under an assumed name at the very Palm Beach hotel his wife had quitted so short an interval before. The letters to Eudora from her mysterious lover were the first things he studied in the solitude of the small room assigned him. He had still no clew to the identity of his wife's lover beyond the name of "Angus." It was signed in a bold hand to one of the compromising notes. The others concluded with the simple initial "A."

Slowly and thoughtfully Philander descended to the foyer of the great hotel. For a moment or two he stood contemplatively at the clerk's desk. Finally he addressed one of the young men busily answering telephone calls and sorting letters behind the marbled bulwarks.

"Anyone here named Angus?"

Philander put the query carelessly, almost jauntily. Yet he dreaded lest the clerk hear the beating of his heart.

"Angus?" echoed the young man blankly, as he handed a card to a bell boy. "Never heard of him."

"Wasn't there a Mr. Angus here last winter?"

Philander received no direct reply to this

query. The clerk had taken a discarded register from beneath his counter.

"You can look for yourself."

Philander turned page after page feverishly. At last he encountered the name of his wife and that of her mother and that of her father. The old gentleman had stayed for a week. The women had lingered. Of any "Angus" there was registered no trace. Meanwhile the young man he had questioned came over to where Philander stood.

"No Mr. Angus ever here," he observed. "The only Angus our people remember is the doctor."

Philander looked up quickly from the book he was fingering.

"Doctor? What doctor?"

"Doctor Angus MacWhortle. He practices in the town."

"Is he a good doctor?"

Philander framed the question in the most careless tone.

"Good as the rest of the boy doctors, I

guess," retorted the clerk jauntily. "The patients hereabouts just think they're sick."

Philander laughed.

"The boy doctors make them think they're well again, eh?"

He turned upon his heel and walked out into the sunny street. He had no difficulty in ascertaining the exact address of Doctor Angus MacWhortle. The proprietor of the first drug store at which he applied gave him the information cheerfully.

"Is he an allopath?" asked Philander. "I have something the matter with my liver and I prefer an allopath."

The druggist's open countenance stiffened slightly.

"I don't know where the doctor got his diploma. He's the youngest physician in the place."

As Philander rang the doctor's bell and took a seat in his waiting room a sense of having run the quarry down brought relief from the long strain he had endured. The doctor himself emerged in almost no time. Angus MacWhortle was a typical boy doctor—alert, well groomed, voluble. His sack suit fitted him within an inch of his life. The flower in his buttonhole was as fresh as a drop of dew in the morning. His voice had all the assurance of Galen's. His manner proclaimed an adamantine self-confidence. His dignity seemed as impenetrable as that of Socrates drinking the hemlock or of Vesalius lecturing on anatomy.

Philander lost no time in complaining of most complicated symptoms. The boy doctor, having extracted a silver cigarette case from one of his many conspicuous pockets, listened with owl-like gravity.

"Auto-intoxication!" he diagnosed suddenly.

He produced a prescription blank and, with a flourish like that of Cæsar stepping upon the shore of Britain, filled it in. Philander received the paper deferentially.

"Doctor," he remarked, "I am amazed by

your insight at first glance into the nature of my case——"

He interrupted himself with a well acted start of surprise. He had allowed his eye to rest upon the prescription, now held in front of him.

"What a coincidence!" exclaimed Philander, his countenance expressing the emotions appropriate to the mental condition of a person taken completely by surprise. "I see, doctor, that you are the writer of the mysterious letter I found in my bedroom at the hotel this morning."

He took from his pocket one of the notes addressed to his wife. Concealing the contents of the communication with his hand, and holding it out so that the doctor could read only the signature, the husband inquired:

"That's your writing, isn't it?"

There was no denying the evidence. The prescription and the epistle were in the same bold penmanship.

"There, there, doctor," said Philander, handing over the compromising document. "You would be well advised in burning that letter. I don't want to pry into your private affairs, but I suppose I may confess that I read the thing through. I didn't know whose it was."

The face of the boy doctor colored with confusion. He seized the bit of paper with a forced chuckle and thrust it into a drawer of the desk at which he sat.

"That was an indiscretion of mine," he faltered. "Of course, I oughtn't to have written like that to a married woman."

The heart of Philander leaped within him. He could go to the divorce court with a sense of perfect security.

"Don't be too severe upon yourself," he brought himself to say, in a jaunty tone still. "You are young and handsome, my dear doctor, and I'm not surprised to learn that pretty women force themselves upon you."

He gave the boy doctor a sly dig in the ribs.

"She didn't force herself upon me exactly," confessed the boy doctor, with an embarrassed laugh.

Philander had taken his hat to go.

"Did you force yourself upon her, doctor?"

The boy doctor looked very wise as he pondered his reply.

"She was one of those women who do not scruple to rouse a man's passions without intending to gratify them."

"Oh!" cried Philander. "I see!"

"When that dawned upon me one night while I was pleading with her," went on the boy doctor, "I grew furious. I laid her across my knee and gave her the worst spanking she ever had in all her vicious life."

Philander raised his hat and held it for a moment before his face. He felt like reeling.

"That," he said, making for the door, was heroic treatment."

"It was the finishing touch," rejoined the boy doctor, bowing his patient out. "She surrendered."

THE FINGER OF FATE

IT was a whole hour beyond the time set for the wedding and the groom had failed to put in an appearance.

The waiting guests, who filled the body of the church, had become the chief victims of a too manifest embarrassment, relieved, it is true, by an occasional ill-bred titter. Here and there one among the guests was making for the door. The bride had been prostrate for the last fifteen minutes upon a couch in the vestry. The agonized mother was applying bay-rum and talking wildly of her poor child.

The unfortunate in question was no less distinguished an advocate of the cause of woman in America than Miss Elizabeth Burdick. This beautiful girl of twenty-six had filled the continent with her fame long before she organized that interminable procession of her sex which required three hours to pass a given point in one great metropolis. But the crusade with which the name of this gifted young lady had especially associated itself in the public mind had to do with the standards of morality.

Miss Elizabeth Burdick clamored fron many a platform that those standards must be the same for both sexes. A woman, Miss Burdick would exclaim, waving the exquisite arms which were no less conspicuous a feature of her platform manner than the burning words she used, a woman must insist upon the same purity in her husband's past life that he would exact in her own.

Behold her now prostrate upon a couch in a church vestry while a thousand wedding guests waited and wondered!

But Miss Elizabeth Burdick arose suddenly to the full height of her tall perfection of figure. She thrust bay-rum and iced water alike from her. With a deprecatory gesture she faced the agitated group. Relatives and bridesmaids crowded about the sofa.

"There is not the least occasion for all our fears," she observed composedly, at last. "Nothing has happened to Richard."

"I could give him a good thrashing!" The minatory exclamation emanated from the grim-visaged brother of the bride. "His explanations must be satisfactory or——"

Elizabeth extinguished this threat with a look. She was a young lady of the type known as dominating. Before another word could be said on either side, the best man, disheveled and panting, had dashed into the vestry.

"It's all right!" exclaimed the newcomer. His face literally steamed from the pores opened by a run through the streets on a summer morning. "Dick'll be here."

He could say no more. Elizabeth, quite recovered from a temporary faintness caused by the suspense, was alone collected enough to offer the hard-pressed youth a place on the sofa. He fell into it.

"Dick saved a girl from drowning as we crossed on the ferry," went on the best man, talking in gasps still. "She must have been going down for the third time. The doctors worked over her before they thought of Dick. But he's all right now."

"Where is he?"

"At the station-house. They'll bring him here as soon as he gets dry clothes."

The aged rector began to don a surplice. The organ pealed. The story had found its way out among the guests in the body of the church. The mother of the bride adjusted her smart hat. The bridesmaids rearranged the ribbons of Elizabeth's dress. She stood like a statue, pondering the adventure.

"The bridegroom!"

The exclamation had burst from the lips of an impatient bridesmaid, peering through an aperture in the vestry door.

"I suppose there's no use of our going

around to the front of the church again and coming in by the main door?"

It was the bride's mother who put this query. Her voice scarcely concealed a natural vexation. A ceremony carefully rehearsed was completely disarranged.

"No."

Elizabeth spoke in a tone quite peremptory. Her mother looked blankly at the clergyman. Elizabeth broke in again:

"Have Dick come in here."

There was no gainsaying a young woman of this bride's well-known decision of character. The best man, recovered by this time from his exhaustion, went out into the body of the church. In a trice he returned with the groom. This wedding, decidedly, was proceeding in defiance of all etiquette.

Once within the vestry, Richard, without a word of greeting to any one else, hastened over to his betrothed. The name of Elizabeth had barely escaped his lips when an inexplicable something in the expression of

her eyes halted him.   He faced her in
mute confusion.   Elizabeth was the first
to break a silence which for all present was
charged with positively electrical effects.

"So you have made a hero of yourself
again, Dick?" began Elizabeth in her coolest
tone.   "Is the young lady out of danger?"

"Quite," put in the best man, for the
groom was obviously still agitated by the
morning's crisis.   "Her people took her away
before I left.   She's Annie Leslie, by the
way—you know her."

At mention of the name, a look was
exchanged between Elizabeth and her
lover, a look very keen and searching on
her part.

"Annie Leslie," echoed Elizabeth.   "I
know her—the lawyer's pretty daughter.
You've met her before to-day, Richard."

The fact that she called her lover "Richard," instead of using the familiar "Dick,"
struck them all.   It had a visibly disconcerting effect upon the young man himself.

"Yes," he said slowly; "I've met Miss Leslie once or twice only, at dances."

But the mother of the bride now refused to tolerate any further delay in the ceremony. The clergyman himself was manifesting impatience.

"The wedding march," he hinted, "is playing."

Elizabeth faced the old man quietly.

"There will be no wedding."

She spoke as if the announcement were the most ordinary thing in the world.

"No wedding!"

Her mother and her lover exclaimed in chorus. The clergyman stood dumfounded. The bridesmaids huddled in a corner.

"Your wedding," interjected Elizabeth's brother at last, "can't be postponed at this time of day."

Elizabeth had given no heed to the emotions inspired by her determination. Her veil was already thrown aside. Richard, stricken as by a blow, caught her hand. She retreated through the door that led from the vestry into the tiny garden behind the church. They faced one another alone there.

"Annie Leslie," said Elizabeth, "will never forget her debt to you."

Richard looked at his betrothed inquiringly. He was an ordinary young man—very. The great things of life went on over his sensible head, especially when they involved the point of view of the modern woman.

"I've only spoken to her three times in my life," he said. "Besides——"

"Do you remember the terms of our engagement?" interrupted Elizabeth. "I told you I would live single until I met a man who could give himself to a wife with a soul as virginal as my own—a past as clean."

"Then you doubt me, Elizabeth?"

"No—you have assured me that you can come to a wife with a past as spotless as her own should be. I believe you. Otherwise I could never have promised to be your wife."

"If you fancy there has ever been any-thing between her and me——"

"Not for a moment. But you have saved another woman from death. That woman will love you for it. I would never marry a man in whose life there is an unfinished romance."

In another moment she was gone.

THE MEASURE OF ALL THINGS

WHEN it transpired that the beautiful Mrs. Hetherington was to take the witness stand on that particular morning, the languishing interest of all New York in the Dike trial was stimulated prodigiously.

Dike had involved himself in financial escapades and, if found guilty, it must go hard with him. Yet there was nothing in his case, sensational though it seemed, to differentiate it from the nine days' wonder that went before or the nine days' wonder that came after. The unexpected appearance of Mrs. Hetherington in the character of an important witness provided just the touch of color to catch the general eye, which had only blinked as yet amid the mists of the Dike case.

For Mrs. Hetherington, wife of one of New York's Wall Street princes, was not only the acknowledged leader of society but the acknowledged beauty of the metropolis as well. Precisely as the classic face and Naiad airs of Helen brought home to Poe the glory that was Greece, did Mrs. Hetherington seem no less essential in one's general idea of the great city than its sky line or Tammany Hall. Her beauty worked such miracles that merely to be known as the husband of Mrs. Hetherington atoned completely for the long, unlovely past of the mature financier whose name she bore. Not that the spell of this lady's fascination exerted itself solely through the depths of a pair of eyes or the calm repose of sloping brows above them or the delicate play of red, red lips revealing white, white teeth. Mrs. Hetherington had a mind as well as a body and a heart as well as a mind. The exact tailoring of her skirt was never more becoming than the fine distinction of her speech or the

sweetness of her manner. Merely to realize that one was a Mrs. Hetherington's fellow creature afforded the most stimulating
sense of how high one had risen in the scale
of evolution.

No wonder the criminal court building
was thronged, on that particular morning, as
the supreme event of the Dike trial mobil-
ized an army of reporters, of photographers,
of deputies. The general public emerged
somewhat slimly from the battle for ad-
mission to the great white chamber, packed,
as the hour approached, like a subway train
on a wet morning. The first days of the
trial had confirmed a general impression of
the dilatoriness of justice. Everybody had
been late in appearing, even the prisoner.
How different now! The spectators crowded
every available inch to which the flimsiest
pretext could afford access fully half an hour
before even a juryman was on hand. Had
the talesmen only known who was to be a

witness, how swiftly that box might have been filled!

A quick stirring about of court attendants precipitated a sudden thrill. This long monotony that killed would relieve itself at last! Necks craned themselves. A pair of dull green folding doors at the upper extremity of the pillared chamber parted.

The district attorney entered.

Enviable man! His was to be the privilege of addressing Mrs. Hetherington face to face. With what an indiscreet fidelity his consciousness of that rare circumstance was reflected in the dignity of his strut! Yet who could gaze at him just then, barbered like a Brummel, without a feeling that the rare glory of his career entitled him to the high reward that was to be his this day? The district attorney was as young as he was brilliant. The great rewards of his profession were just ahead. The public service he had rendered entitled him to confront even a Mrs. Hetherington with all the glamour if

not all the insolence of office.   No mediocrity
among the men here contemplating him as
he peered through his glasses could suppress
an unavailing regret.   Right, no doubt, it
was that this limb of the law should have
beauty brought before him, face to face.
He had worked hard and resisted tempta-
tion and risen by rare merit to renown.   Yet
how partially does fortune distribute her
honors and rewards!   That fat little man under the window near the jury box—might
not he, given the opportunity, have distinguished himself in the law sufficiently to face
a Mrs. Hetherington in all the glamour of
success?

But who comes now?   His Honor!   Hats
off there!   Shut that door!   There rises before us the robed majesty of him whose writs
have potency to translate the divine Mrs.
Hetherington from the splendors of her husband's Fifth Avenue palace to the very hub
of the wheel of crime.   Upon the mere order
of this judge, impassive, serene, coldly con-

templative of the subdued agitation everywhere about him now, even a Mrs. Hetherington must grow deaf to the music of her
sphere and listen only to the law. Nay, His
Honor there, robed and erudite, had power
to commit to prison for contempt that perfect child of time herself! Some consciousness of this was manifest as His Honor, hand
at chin, mused sublimely over flowers in a
vase seemingly neglected near his elbow. The
brooding abstraction of the judicial pose de-
ceived no one that morning. The robed majesty of law itself thrilled at its own vision of
Mrs. Hetherington, subpœnaed out of her
firmament like a goddess plucked from the
sky at some behest of Jove's.

Dike, being on trial, was in the dock, of
course. He was taken as the thing inevi-
table, like the presence of the court stenog-
rapher or the light streaming through the
lofty windows. He had been an imposing
figure in finance before the catastrophe. No
one paid particular attention to him now.

He was not the occasion of this agitated con-
course.   He sat motionless, in a colorless
attitude, a colorless suit, insignificant,
unimpressive.

The rappings for order consequent upon
the entrance of His Honor did not subdue
entirely the vague murmur, the shuffling of
the feet here and there, the faint laughter
now and then and the innumerable sounds
evoked by the presence of this swarm within
four walls.   Somebody had been sworn.   A
lawyer had repeated a question.   There was
a gruff admonition to "Speak up, officer!"
from a court attendant to a uniformed witness connected with the police.   Then, quite
suddenly, all became as still as death.

The fact had dawned slowly, subtly, upon
the general mind that Mrs. Hetherington
was in the court room.   No one, apparently,
had seen her enter.   Yet there she sat, well
forward, near the table reserved for the use
of counsel, with a lady of much greater ma-
turity than herself at her side.   There was

a sort of wonder in the air at the self-effacing manner of Mrs. Hetherington's entrance. She had risen o'er the scene silently like the moon beaming upon the waters of a troubled lake and sending them to sleep. They had anticipated her arrival in grandeur, stepping in an unutterable brilliance to bedazzle them. The throng had expected to have to make a lane through itself for the progress of a heavenly form. Instead, there she was, a surprise—no thunder in the index, but a quiet and insensible coming, like that of dawn.

Mrs. Hetherington, therefore, resembled Niagara in that the first impression, after all that had been said of her, was one of disappointment. But as the second and the third and the fourth contemplation of the falls infuse the mind with a sense of their sublimity, so now they who gazed furtively and repeatedly at that cheek, supported by that hand, drank deep draughts of beauty and delight. One felt that the personality of

Mrs. Hetherington was a pervasive essence, that the light of her countenance shone for a favored few, that the beauty at which all New York gaped with a reverence new and strange was held unspotted from the world. Over the aspect of Mrs. Hetherington, in short, was that indefinable quality of quietness which gives supreme distinction.

There was a sound between a sigh and gasp when the court attendant, betraying by his manner his sense of the spectacular— since merely to be privileged to bawl the name of Mrs. Hetherington was to enjoy a fleeting, fugitive sublimity—called the witness of the day. There fell at once from perfect shoulders a full length coat of heavy black broadcloth and the beauty stood forth, erect. Again that sound between a sigh and gasp met a swift extinction in the rap for order. She advanced with all the brightness of a spirit to the isolated pinnacle of the witness stand, fixing ethereal eyes on all below. With what a complete inevitability

when a loud voice interposed objection.
Counsel for the prisoner insisted upon knowing the meaning of all this irrelevancy. The
district attorney begged to remind the court,
in a very polished manner, that this line of
examination brought out an essential fact.
But all realized, as the brilliant prosecutor
drew himself up to his full height, that his
mellifluous tone was assumed for the benefit
of Mrs. Hetherington, that the rose in his
coat was worn to catch the eye of Mrs. Hetherington, that the official importance of his
manner was a reaction to the stimulus of
Mrs. Hetherington. In the same subcon-
scious fashion was it seen that the judicial
dignity was especially impressive, when His
Honor had to pass upon the point, with an
eye single to the presence of Mrs. Hetherington. There was at work here the same
palpable yet unseen influence which caused
the plain clothes man at the door to enforce
discipline with virtuous severity. One could
hear the breathing of the asthmatic juryman

when the court decided in awful majesty
that Mrs. Hetherington need not answer.
To think that there could reside in the Constitution or out of it power so absolute as
to be able to decide that a Mrs. Hetherington need or need not answer! The judge
sat back in his robe and gazed upon the
hushed assembly in conscious greatness.

Counsel for the defense resumed his seat
in triumph. There had been no great purport, seemingly, in the question challenged.
But who would omit an opportunity to bring
to the notice of a Mrs. Hetherington the circumstance that he lived and breathed? Were
not those combats of the Greek heroes adown
the windy plains of Troy a consequence of
their knowledge that from some high tower
the beautiful Helen beheld their prowess?
The district attorney resumed his examination of the witness with a mortified perception that the prisoner's counsel was swelling
visibly under the eye of Mrs. Hetherington.
All thought of the possible effect upon the

now, "the society of the most obscure member of the bar, if his qualities appealed to
me, would be far more enjoyable from my
standpoint than that of the greatest lawyer
living."

So quietly were the words uttered, so naturally did they arise out of the nature of the
question just put her, that for nearly a full
minute the force of the bomb Mrs. Hetherington had exploded under his case escaped
the district attorney.   Not so with His
Honor on the bench.   He wilted at once.
Why were they there that morning in all
the pomp and circumstance of legal battle
but the better to impress the eye and mind
of beauty?   Now they learned that the greatest among them, the most successful lawyer
who ever lifted himself from a village office
to the post of adviser to corporations, was
no more to Mrs. Hetherington than the pale
and shabby student at the school of law. The
strutting district attorney was nothing to
Mrs. Hetherington.   The black-robed high

priest of the Constitution there on the bench was nothing to Mrs. Hetherington. Yet what, in its essence, is life, what is ecstasy, but the power to impress Mrs. Hetherington, the power to attract the wandering glance of her eye, the possession of the charm that fascinates her? Success at the bar means wealth, honor, a seat upon the Supreme Court bench, but it is all as dust to Mrs. Hetherington. The face of His Honor had grown haggard. He met the look of the district attorney and saw there the sudden and swift perception of her meaning which made these men fellow sufferers. Not, to be sure, that Mrs. Hetherington had deliberately aimed an arrow to wound them. She spoke sincerely, simply, replying in good faith to a direct question without reservation of any kind. The man of law had brought his martyrdom upon himself.

Again that sound between a sigh and gasp revealed the perfect appreciation of that intent audience. Every man among them was miserable from sympathy with the district attorney, aching with pity for the judge. Mrs. Hetherington had opened with the lightning flash of her reply a whole vista in the inky night of human experience. "Why are we?" the great poet asks, and must not the reply be: "For Mrs. Hetherington"? Do not we who are men strive and live and hope for Mrs. Hetherington, cultivate the qualities that charm Mrs. Hetherington? Who would win an empire, pile Pelion upon Ossa, climb the sky, if feats like these paved no path to the favor of Mrs. Hetherington, if they forced her merely to suppress her yawn of boredom? What man, on the other hand, would not dance like a baboon for a kiss from Mrs. Hetherington, paint his visage black for her delight or run yelling into some primeval forest if that could fascinate her? How Mark Antony of old revealed his serpentine guile in abandoning the empire of the world, though it was his to seize, and set-

ting off in pursuit of his Mrs. Hetherington!

Slowly the district attorney came to himself after the first tremendous shock of these
reflections. The judge, more aged, was cowering and shivering in his wrinkled robe.
There were no eyes for either now in that
crowded chamber. Every gaze concentrated
itself upon the form of the prisoner in the
dock. There was the man whose qualities
appealed to Mrs. Hetherington, for there
was the man she had invited again and again
to her dinners. There was the man whose
conversation had delighted Mrs. Hetherington, for she had referred to her admiration of
his wit. There was the man who held the
wandering eye of her beauty, who brought
the smile of pleasure to those rose-red lips—
the man who meant something to Mrs. Hetherington. Before she testified to this tremendous purport there was no man in all
that court so lost and hopeless as to exchange
places with the prisoner. Now the accused

had become the cynosure of all eyes, greater than the district attorney, more honored than the judge, the envy of the jury—and in his serene consciousness of these things Dike sat in that dock smiling, redeemed and glorified.

THE MUSTACHE

I COULD not have been more than twenty-five when I undertook to lead the dignified Mrs. Graftly Lex from the path of virtue.

She was fifteen years my senior, and the wife of that distinguished federal judge whose injunctions were no less notorious than the increase in his wealth after his elevation to the bench. The matronly Mrs. Lex presided over a dignified household comprising, in addition to the servants, her thirteen-year-old son, and, naturally, herself. The judge himself one could leave out of account. He was a cipher in his own home. The wizened and bewhiskered little jurist, in black robe and spectacles, was, nevertheless, a formidable figure on the bench. He ruled the bar of his district as Tarquin ruled the Romans. There seemed nothing on the earth, in the waters below and the heavens above, which could not be brought within the scope of one of his own innumerable injunctions. He could subdue a court room filled with people by the mere thunder of his frown while he committed a dozen hapless wights to the penitentiary for approaching a railroad in defiance of his writs. Few who gazed upon the countenance of the distinguished jurist—who narrowly escaped elevation to the United States Supreme Court itself—could dream that in his own domestic circle he became no less egregious a nullity than those acts of Congress which he regularly declared unconstitutional and void. Judge Lex revenged himself for being a cipher at home by playing the despot on the bench. There seemed always in my mind so subtle a relation between his inconsequentiality at his own table and the unchallenged absolutism of his judicial sway that to this hour

York Harbor rather than the Turkish heaviness of the duenna. The lady's eyes were large, oval and appealingly dark. They had that appetizing chastity of expression which one inevitably associates with the look of Lucrece in repose. Every line exploited by her perfectly corseted figure, however "forced" it might seem in a ball gown, was as impeccable as if Phidias had carved it.

There still ring in my ears as I write the low but deep tones of the jurist's wife. She belonged to the positive and affirmative order of human beings. Determination manifested itself in even the length and straightness of her white Greek nose and the egglike accentuation of her chin. Mrs. Lex had a trick of emphasizing whatever she said with some appropriate movement of her pronounced shoulders. She never conducted a discussion. She literally shouldered it. The slope of this portion of her figure was eloquent, but its language was as chaste as ice and wholly as

dignified as the Roman Senate. Nineteen
centuries of Christian civilization were
summed up in each gesture of those cold,
plump shoulders. They lacked the tigerish
grace of Cleopatra's flesh. Not a hint of the
sensual was ever conveyed by their disturbed
repose. I never beheld them without a con-
viction that lips as ardent as mine became
whenever those shoulders assailed me
through the agonizing yoke of her corsage
must be frozen by the contact of a kiss. Yet
I ached for those shoulders as the senses of
Othello ached at the sight of Desdemona in
her whiteness.

The supreme physical enticement of Mrs.
Lex, however, was her mustache. It was the
lightest, the silkiest of down, clinging tenderly to the perfection of her upper lip in all
the repose of that moonbeam which Shakespeare makes to sleep upon a river bank.
All the commentators have admired the ravishing aptness of that word "sleep" in its so
poetical expressiveness, but it took on for

me a finality of significance when I dreamed of my lady's mustache asleep above her mouth. The French, I know, are more sensitive to this lurking loveliness. Their poets revel in the leger duvet, as they call it, which can become, in its more delicate manifestation, the most angelical feature of the feminine face. For the mustache of Mrs. Lex lacked all coarseness. There are, to be sure, women who can never be mustached with grace, precisely as there are women who cannot smoke a cigarette without forfeiting the divinity of sex. But the countenance of Mrs. Lex rejoiced in that bold and brave beauty which derives emphasis and distinction from the sheer daring of Nature's experiment in penciling her lip.

It was this mustache of hers, then, which drove me to madness. If I sat opposite her at dinner, my eye was lured inevitably from the light of her shoulders to the shadow upon her lip. Mrs. Lex had a trick of sipping her champagne with a certain birdlike tim-

idity—revealing to an eye so jealous as mine
how she dreaded the invasion of her mustache by the moisture. There were times
when, despite the utmost care, some drop of
the drink lingered indiscreetly. It had then
to me all the beauty of that diamond dew
which freshens the tender grass at early
morn. Mrs. Lex never failed to extinguish
the jewel with a white napkin. Oh! to have
been that champagne drop upon that silky
down.

"I can't understand," I heard my sister
say once, "why Pauline does not use a depilatory for that lip of hers."

I could not have been more stunned were
I a pilgrim to Mecca overhearing a sneer at
the prophet's tomb. In another instant my
whole being seemed dissolved by a fire of
esctasy. The thought crossed my mind that
the hair on my lady's lip isolated her as the
deep moat secluded Marianna in her grange.
What bold lovers might not have addressed
themselves to Mrs. Lex but for the disillu-

sionizing effect of her mustache. And what drove them back lured me on!

I went home at once to make a sonnet of the conceit, for I am by way of being a poet of passion. Phryne has come to life in my verse. I have done into odes, lyrics and even hymns every fire that consumed Sappho and every frenzy of Lesbia, Semiramis, Cleopatra, Aphrodite—the sublimest indiscretions of all these and more have inspired me. Nay, it was on account of my poetry that Mrs. Lex singled me out especially among the innumerable members of a social circle distinguished for its æsthetic and intellectual tone. The lady professed herself shocked, to be sure, by what she was pleased to deem the decadent tone of my verse. I have observed, however, in the course of a very successful career as a poet of passion, that the impeccable respectability of a wife and mother by no means disqualifies her as a discriminating and appreciative critic of powers like mine. The appearance of my first volume—it went

to a third edition, by the way—swelled my
mail to gravid proportions with epistles from
the wives and sisters of the very respectables
who form citizens' unions and organize cru-
sades against the social evil. Mrs. Lex was
the only one among them who had a mustache. I dare say my soul is feminine.

I may not suppose that much hackneyed
theme, the length of Cleopatra's nose,
thrilled Pascal, who first referred to it, as
the silken fringe of my lady's lip thrilled me
while I indicted my sonnet on it. I spent a
whole afternoon in polishing the most exquisite lines ever cast by me in the Miltonic
mould. I consecrated the entire octave of
my sonnet to a theme I caught from Hafiz.
"I would give all Samarcand and Bok-
hara," the Persian poet says, "for the Indian
dark mole on the cheek of my lady love."
What, then, must he not have paid for the
herbage of my dear one's lip? I referred to
enchanted butterfles flitting from flower to
flower in quest of perfumes fine enough to

be spun into such a gossamer of love. I
imagined a tear coursing down that cheek
of hers only to be caught and to glitter
through the fringe of an inaccessible lip.
Nor did the fountain of my fancy cease to
play until a whole sonnet sequence had exhausted the theme.

Though I grow to be as old as Goethe, I
shall not outlive the torture of that task. The
dread of compromising the subject by a
single false allusion, the facility with which
even unconsciously I might descend to the
absurd, these considerations haunted me like
so many dragons. I strove, too, for a Diana-
like chastity of utterance. Picking my way
warily amid the pitfalls of anti-climax on
the one hand and mere paganism on the
other, I arrived ultimately at the supreme
test of all. What title should I give my
lines? I had fixed provisionally upon "The
Sentinels," since each line shading that un-
contaminated, cold lip stood guard over my
treasure. An indefinable but distinct sug-

gestion of the absurd warned me, nevertheless, that the figure would not do. For once
my fecund fancy was at fault. In despera-
tion at last, I resolved to submit my problem
to the judgment of a faithful but fantastic
friend, whose suggestions had extricated me
from many a like dilemma in the past.

"I've heard of a poet's sonnets to his mistress's eyebrow," was his first comment.
"These are the first, I'll be bound, ever
penned to a mistress's mustache."

The man who spoke those words was, in
my opinion, the greatest short story writer
in America. Yet he had failed in life, failed
originally and in a fantastic fashion all his
own. Had he been a Frenchman, writing in
France, his fame would have filled two
worlds. The charm of his style, the bold-
ness and originality of his thought, the inexpressible delicacy with which he handled
the most indelicate subject, and, above all,
a deliberate impossibilism of method in his
work which made him rejoice in his own

unavailability as a writer, combined to bring me under the curious spell he could cast upon a nature like mine. I was quite content to accept his verdict upon my sonnet sequence. He laid the manuscript upon the desk in front of him and gazed at me through his immense horn glasses. Then he filled a pipe and puffed in silence, his diverging eyes fixed upon an engraving of Edgar Allan Poe over the fireplace of his study. I was seized by a sudden panic.

"These verses," I faltered, "are they inspired?"

My fantastic friend squinted out of the cast in one of his eyes.

"They will be a classic," he cried, "a classic in one week after their publication. One sonnet in that sequence is a greater contribution to American literature than all Poe put together."

I sighed with a sense of such relief as the Duke of Wellington must have felt at Waterloo when the troops bearing down on him proved to be Blücher's. I trusted the critical insight of my friend implicitly. His enthusiasm seemed to run away with him as he talked on. The cunning of the art with which I had saved the dignity of a theme inherently grotesque and even repellant completely ravished him.

"What," I inquired, "would you suggest as a title?"

His retort was instantaneous:

"Lines on My Lady's Lip."

I leaped to my feet.

"You have been trifling with me!"

"Think it over," he persisted. "If you can think of anything more appropriate in its place—"

He shrugged his shoulders and locked his desk. I could only take my leave of him in anything but a satisfactory frame of mind. As I jumped into a taxicab and was whirled to the home of Mrs. Lex I felt half-inclined to tear my sonnets into tatters and hurl them through the window as if they had been dead pelicans. I was set down at the federal judge's elegant front door before I could summon resolution enough to obey the impulse of my despair.

I found the Lex household in the throes of something like a crisis. The judge had discovered the day before that a recent act of Congress was unconstitutional. The consequence being that he must set out in a special train provided at the expense of a powerful railroad for a tour of observation through some of the most delightful scenery in the land, the judge had requested a number of his friends to make a party. The champagne, the cigars and the general appointment of the special trains in which he toured right and left were provided from the expense funds of a powerful corporation, and the trips invariably lasted several weeks. The expeditions were necessitated by the care the court exercised before selecting a receiver, the process entailing a temporary separation of the judge from his wife. She took not

the least interest in railroading or in railroad travel.

As an adored young friend of the family,
I made my way to the little Japanese room
which the selection of many receivers had
enabled the judge to equip upon a most ex-
pensive scale. A shining touring car drew
up in front of the great portal, and as I
looked down into the avenue I beheld the
wizened little jurist himself trot out. He
caught sight of my face at the pane and
waved me a quick salute. In a trice the
vehicle had sped with him around the corner.

When I turned from the window I found
myself in the presence of the lady with the
mustache. My heart sickened within me as
my eye sought the fine texture of her lip. It
never before had thrilled me so completely
with the subtle significance my sonnets as-
cribed to its miraculous refinement. What
woman in the world, I asked myself, could
emerge in such triumph from a cosmetic ordeal so terrible? Had the hair of Phryne

been upon her lip, would its spell have
worked the wonder upon her judges that
Mrs. Lex now wrought with me? She was
entirely in white, a white flower in the masses
of her heavy head. Plump she was and big,
but it was a graceful magnitude, like the bulk
of the pagoda. What filled me with dismay
was the profanation of which I had been
guilty in essaying any tribute at all to a
beauty so esoteric as to be beyond all worship. Are there not divinities so celestial as
to make even mention of their names by the
most devout worshipper an act of gross ir-
reverence? In the æsthetic, do we not grow
conscious of beauties too refined for appreciation through the faculty of expression? My
sonnets perpetrated the ineptitude of isolat-
ing a physical characteristic from the personality that beautified a blemish by exhibit-
ing it. What if Mrs. Lex wore no mustache
at all and limped instead? The deformity
would become a source of grace in one who
defied the limitations of the flesh through

head of the woman one adores, the glove she has worn and which we cherish as Niobe cherished her children—what consecrates all these apart from the worship given to her of whom each was part? I gazed with a species of horror at the impalpable hair in its sea of milk, aghast at confrontation by such proof of the logical conclusion of love's idolatry. Faugh! I vowed to turn my back on passion and its poetry. I was disenchanted, disgusted. In that very instant my eye reverted to the lip of Mrs. Lex and the old spell was renewed. The subjection of my soul was the more complete from the hideous nature of the ordeal that had freed it for a space.

"You do not answer me," I heard her say in the positive accents more habitual with her. "Sit down here beside me and tell me what's the matter."

I thought of my sonnet sequence as I took my station at her side upon the wide sofa and despair overwhelmed my heart, my mind, my whole spirit.   There are moments, it seems, when the most gifted man that ever breathed begins to doubt his genius.   I lived through such a moment now.   Had I been a truly great poet, I reflected, nothing could have seduced me into such a failure as my verses.   I groaned inwardly as I thought of the opportunity to scatter my manuscript to the winds which only sheer fatuity could have allowed me to let slip.

"I have been working at a poem," I confessed, "and I am tired."

"A poem of passion, of course?"

She had scarcely framed the query when a sudden inexplicable impulse forced me to take the manuscript from my pocket and lay it in her lap.

"What do you call it?" she asked, having unfolded the paper.

I fixed my eyes upon her mustache with the helplessness of the dipsomaniac seeking the bottle.

"Lines on My Lady's Lip."

She lifted her eyes from the sheet in her hand and fell to such perusal of my face as must have disconcerted Ophelia in the most memorable of her scenes with poor Hamlet. My face reddened from confusion. I saw the cheeks of the judge's wife flush markedly. She turned with an obviously awakened curiosity to the sheets of paper. I leaped from my place beside her and walked over to the window. I had to grasp a chair for support.

I lacked the courage to turn my eyes in her direction until, as I calculated, she had been afforded time to study the first sonnet. I beheld a flash of some weird fire in her gaze, but when she saw how my eye was drawn to her lip she covered her mouth with a handkerchief. She went on with the reading. I resumed my vacant review of the interminable procession of vehicles in the street below.

Not until the sound of weeping assailed my ear did I look back once more. Her head was pillowed against the wall and I could

not see her face.   Her hands were pressed
against every feature of a countenance which
in my eyes was integrated around that mustache with all the sublimity of the creative
cunning that has built our planetary system
around the sun.   The spectacle of that white-
robed and magnificent wife and mother shed-
ding tears in consequence of a humiliation
of which my verse had been the instrument
smote me with shame.   In a flash of illumination I beheld the hideousness of the gross
breach of good taste of which I had been
guilty.   Not until the sighs parting her lips
had shot arrows to my heart was it borne
in upon me that the hair upon the lady's lip
was from her standpoint a deformity.   How
oddly opposite is the point of view of the
sexes!   I recalled then the story of a Greek
virgin whose bosom filled every youth with
such fire that she mutilated herself, in dread
lest she be a perpetual object of ridicule.
She was, instead, a perpetual object of
desire.   Here was a modern instance.   What

obscurity of an oracle. I drew upon my
store of learning with reference to the mani-
festations of passion. I reminded her that
mine was the artist soul, the soul that
explores strange sins, old lusts, the isles of
Lesbos and the grottoes of Capri. The lines
upon her lip, I explained, were among those
forgotten spells of passion which the beauti-
fying Greeks succumbed to. They authenticated her mission as my soul's submission to
the mesh and snare of her incantation
authenticated me as poet of passion. That
phrase struck me mute. Was I, after all,
a poet of passion? Had I not wandered off
into some neglected bypath of the flesh,
inhaling the mephitic and miasmatic vapor
of the charnel house of love? Ah! the haunting dread that I never was a poet in any
sense and must figure forever as a classical
case in the literature of the Krafft-Ebing
psychopathy left me as forlorn as the distracted creature I sought to console. In an
agony of shame I flung myself at full length

upon the rug at the feet of Mrs. Lex and hid my face.

"My poor child!"

These words, repeated again and again, brought me out of the valley of the shadow of this death. I opened my eyes to find my head in her lap. She had vainly striven to get me to rise. I lay motionless while she applied her handkerchief to my temples.

"I suppose," I faltered, looking up into that hair upon her lip, "I suppose you will never forgive my bad taste."

She ceased to rub my temples long enough to lose her gaze in the depths of mine.

"Wonderful, wonderful boy!" she cried. "I was so proud when I first read those sonnets to think that they owed their inspiration to myself."

My heart leaped up. The next instant I abandoned hope again at sight of a large round tear traveling slowly from her eye to the divine texture of which my unhappy poem was the hymn.

"Your poem is a miracle of genius," she said. "You have excelled yourself. Shelley himself could not have surpassed the magic of that concluding sonnet."

"What drew the tears from your eyes, then?"

I put the question with a lingering doubt of her perfect sincerity. Yet there was no acting in the enthusiasm of her tone. Mrs. Lex was a lady for whose critical judgment every literary man in the metropolis felt profound respect.

"I shed those tears, my poor boy——"

She stood on the brink of a disclosure. I saw her hesitate. Again my heart made its tremendous leap.

"Tell me," I urged. "I am an artist and therefore I understand everything, and to understand everything is to forgive everything."

She made the plunge.

"I am not the woman you think me," she

confessed. "I am unworthy of the reverence you have paid me."

For the first few seconds I could not drink in the poison of the revelation.

"I have lived life," she said, bending over me as my head still lay in her lap, "and I have loved love."

The hair upon her lip was closer to my eyes than ever it had been before. The disclosure of her past, made with the subtlety of expression that only a poet could at that moment have elicited or understood, steeped my being swiftly in the deep, deep waters of a new bitterness. I had achieved a great poem. There could be no doubt of that. Yet I had founded it upon a betrayal of myself. The prophetic vision of the true seer had not been mine. The tragedy of that thought was like a shadow blackening the lips now so close to my face. The delicate netting of hair seemed coarser. I detected a solitary bristle amid the gossamers.

"That story, then," I ventured, closing my eyes that I might not see her mustache, "connecting your name with the Senator's——"

I heard no reply. Opening my heavy eyes, I saw her head sink yet lower. She was supporting me with her arms. Her head nodded and I could see that she was suppressing a sob.

"Only a great artist like yourself," she murmured, "can understand."

I wanted to shut my eyes. She was weeping afresh, silently, yet copiously. The tears, streaming discreetly yet plentifully, were caught in the growth which had led me to immortalize her lip. I saw one stubborn drop shine at the tip of a hair like a lantern outside a house of sin. That any such com·parison could institute itself in my mind just then proved to my dismay how complete was the revolution of my soul. Her mustache, wet with her tears, became to me a bedraggled and loathsome thing. The moisture from her eyes fairly blackened it. Each particular hair, grown gross and heavy to my sense like the flavor of some soured beverage, was to me a whip lashing the naked soul of me.

"My dear, dear boy," she murmured. "How you have suffered."

The grave which she had dug for my sentiment contained no corpse that she could see. With her arms around my form and her lips close to my face, I could merely gaze helplessly as my distracted head pillowed itself in her lap. My one refuge was my eyelids. These I closed with a convulsive shudder. Every hair upon her lip spoke to me now of some stain upon her crimsoned soul. Closed as were my eyes, I could actually see the lips of lovers clinging to her own. The supreme horror was my recollection that the Senator whom I had mentioned had likewise a mustache. The contact of the lines upon my lady's lip with the heavy red bristles beneath the statesman's nose afforded that complete blend of horror with the

laughable which is the touchstone of great
art. I had no longer any doubt that my
present plight was a contrivance of Lucifer's.
I saw this woman's mustache mingling sin-
fully with the hairs upon the lips of innumerable roués, deriving from every fresh contact the aroma of another debauch.   Those
hairs were not, as I had so madly imagined,
sentinels of a delighted spirit, but the stag-
nant marsh in which were bred all the
apocalyptic beasts of forbidden desire.

"Sweet boy!"

She murmured the words in my ears as I
was realizing by the inward light of the
soul how ravishing must be the virginities
and the chastities. Diana, I reflected, could
have worn those lines upon her lip without
a suggestion of the loathsome.   Sin it was
which brings the disgusting recollections,
which makes the mustache of Mrs. Lex reek
with the champagne it had been steeped in,
the smoke of the cigarettes, the burning of
kisses, and above all, age, the long weary

years it had grown and grown without the application of steel or depilatory. I shuddered with disgust.

Then came the last horror of them all. Her lips met mine. The contact was like the march of many crawling spiders. My smooth cheek was not spared. I was very, very young, for a poet of my fame, and I had little need of a razor. The mustache seemed now instinct with a life independent of the woman's. It rasped my skin. I remembered the plight of a traveler in South America waking to find the tarantula traversing his skin, and daring not to move lest some agonizing sting drive him to madness. How clearly, in the light of this revelation from experience, I read the message of the saint who extols the rapture of chastity. There was a subtle and inexplicable spirituality of which I had not caught the thrill. And all the while the lip crawled in its hairy horror from my mouth to my brow and over my closed eyes, bearing foul memories of what that mustache had touched and been touched by. In a spasm of disgust I leaped to my feet and ran from the house. The week had not passed before every literary gazette announced that I had abandoned poetry forever and gone into Wall Street.

MISS DIX

"**M**ISS DIX has promised to marry you!" I echoed in my amazement, turning to young Vernon. "But she has promised to marry me!"

Never before had I seen upon a human countenance an expression of such grief as seemed now to shake the whole foundation of the youth's being.

"Miss Dix," he repeated, slowly and in a tone quite new and strange to me, "has promised to marry—you!"

The words had barely escaped him when the door of my apartment opened and Montague entered.

"The portrait is quite finished!" were his first words. "It is to be exhibited, too, in the gallery of the Arts Club!"

Never had I seen him so radiant. As he

threw aside his hat and cane I exchanged a look with Vernon. I knew at once that the secret between us was not to be broached even to so intimate a friend as Montague. That great artist offered us cigarettes before he spoke next.

"It is a wonderful study of Gloria!"

I experienced a shock at Montague's allusion to Miss Dix by her first name. Something of my feeling doubtless prompted the repetition by Vernon, in accents partly of wonder but mainly of protest, of the name we both adored.

"Gloria! May we see this masterpiece of yours?"

The artist sank back upon the cushions of the great divan before heeding the request.

"I have a bit of news for you," he said.

Montague's words were spoken quietly. The manner of the man seemed oddly grave and dignified. This artist, as magnetic as he was brilliant, seemed instinctively flippant always in speech and in manner. I divined now that the mood upon him was anything but characteristic. A subtle something in his aspect connected the news he had to tell—in my mind at least—with Miss Dix. That idea caused me to steal a look at Vernon. The youth did not heed me. His eyes were concentrated upon the face of Montague. I saw that the impression I had derived was his, too.

"Well," spoke up Vernon, after a minute's complete silence, during which Montague studied the ceiling as he lay prostrate, "what is this wonderful news?"

"I did not say it was wonderful," I heard the artist answer solemnly. "Yet the news is, indeed, wonderful. I am engaged to Miss Dix."

He did not use the name of Gloria this time. When he had ceased speaking he gazed as before at the ceiling and exhaled a quantity of cigarette smoke. I relieved myself with a long gasp, but said no word.

I could hear the deep breathing of young Vernon as he stood by the window. For a second only our looks met. I read there an entreaty that the secret we shared be kept from Montague. The silent appeal was unnecessary. Nothing could have dragged from my lips the revelation that Miss Dix had pledged herself to me only the night before.

"Suppose," Vernon whispered rather than said at last, "suppose we inspect this portrait of Miss Dix."

Montague looked at him in some surprise. The artist had expected a word of congratulation from one or the other of us, I suppose. He turned his eyes upon me, but I purposely busied myself with my hat and coat and stick.

"Very good!" agreed Montague. "We can step over to the studio at once, if you like."

"Did Miss Dix have to give you many sittings?" inquired Vernon, when he had got down to the street. He spoke wistfully, his young face all peaked and pallid.

"She gave me no sittings at all," confessed the artist. "I carry her image in my mind only—and," he added in a moment, "in my heart."

I forgot my own anguish of body and soul in the unutterable pain stamped upon the poor boy's face by Montague's words. We had crossed the street before I could find a theme through the medium of which our talk could be diverted into new courses. I wanted to mention the balmy air, to dwell upon the beauty of a statue fashioned by our mutual friend Sullivan—to speak of anything but the one engrossing subject of Miss Dix. Montague meanwhile led the way up the long and narrow flight of steps to his own door.

"Sullivan!" he exclaimed, pausing with a bunch of keys in his hand.

It was, in fact, the distinguished sculptor. He followed the rest of us into the artist's

immense studio. For the first time in my
experience of Sullivan, he failed to greet us
with a laugh and a witticism.

"I'm very anxious to see this masterpiece
of yours," he remarked, as the artist opened
a skylight in the roof. "I've heard ever so
many men raving over the thing at the
club."

Montague had drawn aside the drapery to
afford a view of the canvas. For the next
two or three minutes no word was spoken by
any of us. The world has long since grown
familiar with Montague's imperishable masterpiece. The eyes of the portrait looked
forth upon us then and there with all the
inscrutable depth of the expression of Miss
Dix. The folds of the hair of Miss Dix
arranged themselves about her brow and
temples on this canvas until one seemed to
catch the very perfume of the living tresses
in their perfection. The supreme success
of Montague in this study of Miss Dix
seemed to me to reside in the mouth. He

had realized it delicately yet vividly, doing justice to every appealing curve without compromising its flawless harmony with the face as a whole. It was such a face as Juliet might have turned in rivalry with the beauty of the moon when Romeo beneath the balcony invoked the winged messenger of heaven for its model.

"Montague," I heard the sculptor say, in subdued tones, when our contemplation of the painting had silently endured for what seemed to me scarcely a minute, although, as I found by consulting my watch, the interval was much more, "Montague, I hope you won't send such a jewel to the gallery to be stared at by the herd."

I glanced up quickly into the sculptor's face. I detected at once in his voice an emotional something present in the tones of young Vernon when he told me he loved Miss Dix. Montague fixed his eyes upon the face of the speaker with something like resentment in his look.

"I may have felt as you did—once," he observed, coldly. "But Miss Dix herself insists that I exhibit her portrait."

The sculptor was plainly surprised.

"I shall ask her," he declared at once, "to permit nothing of the sort."

The manner rather than the matter of his speech, uttered, as it was, in the tone of one having authority, drew our eyes to his face. For a second Sullivan confronted us in an attitude of embarrassment. Then he explained:

"The fact is that Miss Dix and I are—engaged."

He hesitated at the last word. I saw Vernon lean heavily against the wall. Montague stood as rigid as if he had been petrified.

"What is the matter with you?" asked Sullivan, in manifest irritation, finally. "Is there anything so terrible in the fact that I am engaged to Miss Dix?"

"I think," was the only reply he received, and the words issued in faint tones from the lips of Vernon, "I think I shall go to my rooms. I have not been feeling well for some time."

He would have fallen had we not rushed simultaneously to his side. Nothing could have been more disconcerting at that moment than Vernon's illness. This brilliant youth had lately completed a play which justified, in the minds of the few who had read the work, the high hopes of his future entertained by all who knew him. For weeks past he had been busily supervising rehearsals. The first public performance was fixed for that very evening.

"My dear Vernon" I ventured to say, as we bore him to the great divan at one end of the studio, "you simply must be in the theatre by eight o'clock."

He sank upon the pillows with a groan.

"Bother all that!" he cried. "I'm simply not equal to the strain of it to-night."

It required our united exertions to put him in a different frame of mind. I alone had a clew to the poor boy's state. I fancied, when we had got him again upon his feet, that Montague had some slight suspicion of the truth. I evaded the artist's eye, dreading lest he surmise my own ordeal. Sullivan could make nothing of the general mystification in which we were involved.

"I've ordered dinner at the club," he said, as Vernon donned hat and coat. "Afterwards we'll all go to the play."

This had been arranged long before. I had no doubt whatever of the impending triumph in store for young Vernon. His extraordinary genius was still undisclosed to the public, but his few intimates, including Montague and Sullivan as well as myself, had succumbed to this youth's spell from the first day of his appearance among us. In a few hours the city was to ring with his name. Now he stood up before us in the aspect of a man condemned to die.

The four of us made a melancholy dinner party. The club was filled with merry-

makers that night. Many an eye was cast
in our direction. The great experience in
store for the young playwright accounted
to all, apparently, for the nervousness he
displayed. I felt his hand upon my arm just
before the coffee.was served.

"Miss Dix!"

He hissed the name into my ear. I had
but a moment before fancied her present
among a group of diners at the other end of
the room. I looked about quickly.

"She's gone," whispered Vernon. "She
passed through the door just now."

"Have you invited her for to-night?"

I put the query into his ear alone. Vernon
shook his head.

"I thought of having her. But it was she
who inspired the play, who gave me the idea
even——"

He gulped a draught of champagne.

"I understand," was my whispered reply.
"You were not sure of a success and you
feared her presence——"

He nodded quickly and I said no more. Sullivan lighted a cigar and puffed moodily now, while Montague sent for a taxicab.

The theatre seemed crowded as I glanced up and down from the box in which the four of us were placed. It is superfluous to say a word of the play or of that first performance of it. The phenomenal run of the piece in New York, its innumerable repetitions in London and elsewhere have made the name of Vernon one of the glories of the American drama. The youthful playwright sat beside me through it all with sorrow stamped upon his face. To the loud calls for the author at the conclusion of the last act he paid no attention whatever. He simply turned and fled, the three of us following like men possessed.

"So," began Sullivan, the moment we were seated facing one another in the automobile, "we're all engaged to Miss Dix."

Not one of us had a thought for the magnificent triumph Vernon had achieved that

night. It was now upon the verge of midnight. All about flowed the streams of
humanity belched into the lighted streets
from a score of theatres, but we had neither
eyes nor ears for the spectacle. I had
directed the chauffeur to convey us forthwith
to Professor Grimm's. That renowned
medico-psychologist happened to be in the
number of our intimates, and I knew his
habits well enough to have no doubt of finding him in his study. Luckily my order had
passed unobserved by the rest, who took it
for granted that we were conveying Vernon
to his rooms. Sullivan's remarks on the subject of Miss Dix met with no comment from
any of us. Not a word more was said until
we drew up before the expert's door.

"Upon my word!" exclaimed Sullivan,
when he had leaped to the sidewalk, "what
possessed us to drop in on old Grimm?"

I was too busily engaged in assisting Vernon to find a reply. The youth suffered himself to be led up the steps of the brownstone

mansion, where he leaned heavily against Montague until my ring brought a response.

"Bless my soul!" growled Grimm the moment his whiskered and wrinkled visage— for he answered the summons in person— had been thrust through the doorway. "Bless my soul!"

He made no further comment until we were seated at the back of the house in the gloomy study consecrated to his solitude. I lost no time in coming straight to the point. The aged specialist, with whom, as I have hinted, we were all intimate, shrugged his shoulders when I had told my story.

"Don't worry about our friend Vernon," he snorted. "He'll learn before long that there is no Miss Dix."

I stared at Grimm as he filled a villainous pipe. My exclamation coincided with that of Montague.

"No Miss Dix!"

"No Miss Dix!" chimed in the pathologist between energetic puffs. "I've heard of her before, for I've met many an artist. But there is no such female."

"Your mood, doctor," I said, "is a trifle fantastic, isn't it?"

"Not as fantastic as yours," retorted the old man. "But then, you're a poet. That poem of yours—the one that is quoted everywhere, I mean—I suppose you'll tell me it was inspired by Miss Dix."

I flushed to the roots of my hair. The aged scientist had exposed a secret I had meant to lock forever in my own breast.

"I don't mind your having your laugh at our expense, doctor," began Montague, "but——"

"I'm not laughing at you," insisted Grimm, his pipe smoking actively between his teeth; "I'm talking psycho-pathology to you. The trouble is that the four of you are artists. You combined to create Miss Dix out of your own temperaments. When did you first see her?"

The question gave me a thrill. It

occurred to me at once that I had never yet seen Miss Dix alone. She had spoken to me first at the end of a talk I once gave at the Waldorf-Astoria. Our subsequent meetings were indeed frequent—at public dinners, at gatherings to promote woman suffrage in studios. The one delightful evening we ever passed side by side chanced to be on the occasion of a meeting of the Poetry Society. I had yielded to an irresistible impulse then and asked her to become mine forever. I turned swiftly in my chair and faced Sullivan.

"When did you first see Miss Dix?"

My question embarrassed the artist visibly.

"On the opening of the last academy exhibition," he told me in tones so constrained that I forbore to press him further. It was Vernon who spoke next.

"I saw her first at one of your lectures," he confessed in my ear. "I know her only through you."

The words were little more than a whisper, but Grimm overheard every one. He pressed his point home.

"Yes, yes," he interposed, "you know her through him and he knew her through you. That's the way with Miss Dix. She is an evocation of the artist soul. Miss Dix was the mysterious lady of Shakespeare's sonnets. She inspired the sudden outburst of the Athenian genius in the age of Pericles. She was Dante's Beatrice and Petrarch's Laura. Miss Dix caused all the trouble between Shelley and Byron and she was Poe's Lenore. You can't tell me anything about Miss Dix—there never was a Miss Dix and there never will be."

The flow of the scientist's words was checked by the movements of Vernon. He had risen quickly and now confronted old Grimm.

"You're mad!"

The brilliant young playwright hissed the two words as if they were daggers. Grimm removed his pipe from between his lips and grinned.

"Someone's mad," he conceded, "but the world is only beginning to find out who it is. It's art that's mad and Miss Dix has made it so."

I had risen when Vernon spoke, with some vague notion of calming his agitation. Montague took his hat and Sullivan followed the example.

"The old warfare between science and religion," I heard Grimm saying as he walked to the door, "is to make way for a new warfare between science and art. All art is nothing but Miss Dix on canvas, Miss Dix in sonnets, Miss Dix in sculpture and Miss Dix in music. You artists say she exists and you call her Mona Lisa or the Venus de Milo——"

"Good night, doctor!" I called, fumbling with the handle of the front door.

"So you won't believe me!" shouted the old man, growing suddenly hot tempered.

"Good! I'll prove to you that there is no Miss Dix and never was a Miss Dix."

Vernon seemed to catch at the idea as if it were a rope let down to him at the bottom of a well.

"Prove that—yes!" he cried, with more animation than I had supposed him capable of then. "Prove that there is no Miss Dix, and I——"

His utterance grew choked and he leaned heavily against the door. Without a word old Grimm snatched a hat from the rack in the hall and went with us into the street.

An army of stars trooped the sky as we passed on through the silent and deserted side street. A glance at my watch showed that midnight had long come and gone. We were in Sixth Avenue and pacing through its gauntlet of electric lights before another word was uttered. Vernon had pulled himself together and was walking well ahead, with Sullivan and Montague on either side of him.

"Don't worry over the lad," begged Grimm; "he'll be all right by to-morrow morning."

I thought of saying that the rest of us might never get over it, when we seemed engulfed by a sudden tide of humanity. I caught sight of the uniforms of policemen at a corner. The shining brass of a patrol wagon was reflected to my eye as Grimm halted me with a pull at my arm. I signaled to the others, who at once crossed with us to the scene of all this nocturnal activity.

I heard someone in the crowd say something about a raid. There was a spurt of energy among uniformed men in brass buttons, and a movement of the horses harnessed to the patrol wagon. From the depths of a basement we saw human forms emerge and take their places side by side in the official vehicle.

"My God!" cried Vernon, who stood on the outskirts of the throng of humanity. "Miss Dix!"

A murmur of admiration had greeted her appearance between two policemen. Slowly they led her to the brassed wagon, in which she took her place among a dozen of the raided. I saw Vernon leap forward. I was at his side in a second. Then we were halted by a policeman's drawn club.

"You can't get by, mister," said the man in blue, decisively.

"I want to speak to Miss Dix."

The lad spoke feverishly. He signaled to the exquisite figure of the woman whose face had so lately filled us with awe on Montague's canvas. But his gesture passed unnoticed. That face might have been graven in stone, so impassive it seemed now.

"She'll be taken to the night court," I heard the policeman say. "You can talk to her there."

Vernon turned at once. We all followed in hot haste, for the speed of the young man forced the pace. In Broadway a taxicab seemed to make its appearance by a special dispensation of Providence. The five of us squeezed in.

A sensational rumor of the raid had preceded us to the night court. Never had its precincts been so thronged before, surely. For one terrible moment it seemed that we would be excluded by the inexorable man at the door. Old Grimm effected our purpose in the end by means of a message to the blue-coated official who held the throng to some standard of order within.

"What's it all about?" I heard the pathologist ask of the grizzled veteran of police who showed us forward.

"They've got the Dix woman."

This was said solemnly. Old Grimm looked innocent.

"The Dix woman?"

The inquiring tone brought out a flood of information. The Dix woman was notorious. She it was who inspired the vice of the Tenderloin. She directed the white slave traffic. She hired the disorderly houses. She devised the methods of sin. She eluded the police. She had powerful friends. She had been caught at last.

There ensued, when our reservoir of official information had exhausted itself, a long suspense, broken for me at intervals by the occasional whispers of Grimm to the effect that there was no Dix woman.

A shuffling of feet at the bar, a loud call for order and the emergence of a black-robed figure on the bench rendered the opening of court a welcome relief. Only Grimm, of our party, seemed at ease.

A door opened on the right. One by one, the figures of the prisoners appeared in the glare of light from the ceiling. The activity ceased as swiftly as it had begun. There was a meaningless pause.

"Bring in the Dix woman!"

The command emanated from the throat of one of the bluecoats. Again that door gaped. Every eye was on it. We saw it close. We saw it open again.

A lone policeman emerged conspicuously. He whispered to the attendant at the desk, who whispered to the clerk, who whispered to the magistrate. The judicial dignitary gasped.

"Escaped!"

The magistrate repeated the words in a louder tone. He said it yet again. The last syllable seemed to have the volume of a thunder clap and the magisterial countenance had the blackness of the cloud. We saw the desk pounded by the figure in the black robe. We heard indignant words. The notorious Dix woman had escaped! Never, vowed His Honor, had the law been outraged by a more flagrant instance of police imbecility and incapacity. The man in blue bowed his head to the storm. He was told that he would be reported, dismissed from the force, disgraced forever.

"But that woman will be found!" bellowed His Honor. "The city will be scoured for her."

Grimm turned to me and grinned in my face.

"That woman won't be found!" he whispered in my ear. "There never was a Dix woman and there never will be."

I glanced back uneasily at Vernon, who sat immediately behind me. Montague and Sullivan, on either side of the youth, seemed not to have heard what the old pathologist had whispered. I tried to attract the attention of my friends, but they paid no heed to my signals. Their attention was concentrated upon the bench. The magistrate still pounded.

"Here's the Dix woman, your Honor!"

The exclamation issued from the lips of a perspiring policeman. He stood hat in hand before the magistrate, upon whom the intelligence exercised a soothing effect. The door opened once again. A woman, escorted by two bluecoats, was led before the bench. I heard the court clerk announce the name of the prisoner as Dix.

"That is not Miss Dix!"

Vernon had leaned forward to say this. The professor caught the words as I did.

"Of course it's not Miss Dix!" snapped old Grimm. "But the police will swear it's Miss Dix to save their jobs. They know there never was a Miss Dix and never will be one. Didn't they produce a spurious Helen after the capture of Troy and didn't the Greeks take her home under the impression that she was the genuine article?"

THE FORBIDDEN FLOOR

I

It may be—I do not say that it is—but it may be that it is as unreasonable to require a ghost to appear in an atmosphere of cold skepticism as to require a photograph to be developed in a blaze of sunlight.—Mgr. R. H. Benson.

"THIS stairway," she concluded, with the graceful movement of her long, white arm, which seemed no less natural than the musical quaver in her tone—"this stairway leads to my son's rooms."

For the first time in my brief experience of Mrs. Bowers the quiet serenity of expression which constituted one of the many charms of her beautiful face left it utterly.

The large, deep-blue eyes were visible to

me now only through the screen of drooping lashes. The coils of her glorious white hair were beneath my eyes. She had bent her head with the manifest purpose of concealing some too poignant emotion.

For the space of a minute I had to gaze vacantly at the sudden whiteness of her smooth brow, the quick curl of her exquisite red lip. The change from the repose of manner which made the mere presence of this lady soothing disconcerted me.

I felt a sudden wonder that one so fair to behold should have remained a widow. Then I glanced over my shoulder at the stairway.

Access to the wide flight of waxed wood steps was denied by a barred gate of curiously wrought bronze reaching from the floor to perhaps the height of my waist. My eye followed the stairway to the landing above. It was that of the top floor.

Like everything connected with this old colonial mansion, the banisters were built upon a massive scale. They wound about the turn of the stairway at the top floor and were lost to view behind heavy green curtains of velvet. As I gazed curiously, I heard the notes of one of Beethoven's most mystical compositions.

My ears had but begun to drink in the rhythm when I experienced an uncanny shock of what I can only call suspicion. It was the sort of sensation I had had when, years before, I felt intuitively the presence of a person hiding in my room. The instinct had not misled me then. I was sure it did not mislead me now.

There was no shadow of doubt in my mind that behind the curtain above us at the head of those stairs lurked an eavesdropper. There seems to linger in things material some trace of the personality of him or of her by whose daily contact they once derived their atmosphere or their essence.

I know not what term may best denote the subtle influence of the individual upon surrounding objects. A suggestion of it came vividly into my mind as my eye roved up the stair and was halted by the curtain. All objects here conveyed their message as plainly as a whisper in the ear.

The half light seemed charged with intimations of an unrevealed but not unsuspected presence. The very floor beneath my feet, like the ceiling overhead, was telling some story, and telling it in a way that thrilled. But that lady at my side was moved, apparently, only by the music floating to us from behind the curtain.

"That is Arthur himself playing," I heard her whisper.

I withdrew my eyes from the stairway and gazed once more at the widow's pale face. Mrs. Bowers was always lovely to look upon, but each time she alluded to her son the light in her deep-blue eyes made her seem young despite the snowy hair massed upon her brow.

She withdrew noiselessly from the gate

at the foot of the stairway, and I had no alternative but to follow. We were in the library below before she said another word.

"You shall meet my son at dinner; that is, if he comes down to dinner."

She hesitated. Her soft hand clutched the handkerchief she held.

"You will not mention that gate to my son?"

Her eyes framed a piteous appeal to me as she asked that. I bowed my head, fearing lest a word might wound her.

"My son is a little—fanciful." She brought out that last word by a visible effort. "No one goes to the top floor—not even myself—except the housekeeper."

I had no time to reply before she fled, leaving me to work among the books. Instead of delving at once among the mass of papers upon the library table, I mused for some minutes upon the mystery of the forbidden floor.

I had never seen the young man who held

such undisturbed possession there. My own
connection with this household had begun
only a day or two before. My presence in
the mansion was due to the anxiety of Mrs.
Bowers to give the world an authentic biography of her late distinguished husband.

His career had been no less varied than
it seemed brilliant.   The splendor of his
Civil War record caused his election to conspicuous public posts.   He had served his
native land in her diplomatic corps.   Great
financial enterprises owed their success to
his administrative genius.

One of his speeches was so perfect a specimen of a certain kind of oratory as to have
found a place in the school readers.

The widow of this brilliant man had been
shocked by what purported to be accurate
versions of her husband's career. These had
been exploited in various periodicals and
newspapers in a fashion calculated to dis-
credit the motives of the dead man at one
great crisis in the nation's destiny.

Mrs. Bowers burned to vindicate the good name of him whose memory was to her so sacred. The executors of her husband's estate had made me a most flattering offer to undertake the task of a biographer.

The prospect of a few months in the country amid surroundings so conducive to my personal comfort was too tempting to resist, quite apart from all considerations respecting the liberal stipend offered by the widow.

This was the second day of my residence in the Bowers mansion. I had no clue to the character of the widow's son. I gathered from the somewhat vague details supplied by the reticent lawyer who engaged me in the city that Arthur Bowers was a gifted but somewhat fantastic young man, who wrote poetry and painted.

From the elderly housekeeper who showed me to my room on the night of my arrival I derived the additional impression that he kept much to himself. It now appeared that he barred himself against intrusion behind a gate. For the extreme beauty of the widow I had been totally unprepared.

I had expected to find an ancient dame living in the past. I found, instead, a gracious lady, white-haired, to be sure, but seductive in the willowy lightness of her figure and irresistible through the fresh beauty of her face.

It was time to dress for dinner when my preliminary inspection of the late general's correspondence was completed. The intimacy of the relations revealed in the letters with men who have made our country's history was astounding.

It was obvious that a biography of the eminent statesman would prove highly sensational, disclosing, as it must, unsuspected factors in the growth of our republic from an isolated nation to a position of supreme importance among the great powers of the world.

One or two episodes of historical impor-

tance with which these letters were concerned
made it imperative to consult not only the
widow, but the son, before any details could
be made public. I had not spent two hours
in a study of the documents before me, yet
I was already in possession of political
secrets for which many a sensational publication would pay considerable sums. My
appreciation of this fact made me a little
uncomfortable. What if the facts now in
my possession were disclosed prematurely
through some one's indiscretion? I might
be accused of betraying a confidence. In
much perplexity I restored the bundles of
letters to the great desk at which I worked.
I must consult the dead man's son without
delay.

As I left the library for the dining-room
my ear caught the strains of music from the
top of the house. I halted at the head of
the stairs. The keys of a piano were evidently responding to the hand of a master.
I could have listened for an hour.

The air was quite unknown to me, although the rhythm vaguely suggested the Italian school. The thought flashed through my mind that I might be listening to one of the young man's own compositions. In that event, Arthur Bowers was a genius. My eye met that of the old housekeeper.

She stood mutely and with the rigidity of a statue, gazing down at my upturned face. I felt a moment's annoyance. This old lady might be one of those disagreeable people whose aptitude for watching unobserved suggests a tendency to be sly.

"Master Arthur won't be down to-night, sir," she said.

Her tone was hushed. Her manner was respectful enough. I could not help thinking, as I studied her lined face, that she alone had access to the forbidden floor. With her last word she disappeared, and I went on down.

Whatever intentions I had formed to discuss the matter perplexing me with Mrs.

Bowers herself were foiled by the presence
of guests. One of these was a graceful
young lady, dark-eyed and tall, with a
becoming gravity of manner. The other
was her father, a local judge, pompous and
little, with that self-assertiveness which a
career on the bench does so much to develop
in a man.

"So you're Mr. Roegers, are you?" he
snapped, seizing my hand. "Glad to meet
you. I hope you'll turn out a right account
of my old friend, the Senator."

With that he dropped my hand, or rather
flung it from him. I was so extremely
amused by his swelling port that I at once
forgave the bruskness of this little judge.
One could have forgiven anything in a man
with such a daughter.

Miss Miggs soothed where her father
ruffled. She deferred where he played the
bully. But she was hopelessly eclipsed by
the dazzling beauty of the white-haired
woman. Mrs. Bowers wore a décolletté

dress of black and gold, from which her
shoulders emerged like the petals of a lily.
Her perfect arms were in fluttering motion.

Her manifest regret at the absence of her
son lent to the smile with which she favored
us in turn an inexpressible melancholy that
sweetened her face like a perfume. I understood that the judge was a widower. I wondered if he could be courting our hostess.

"So Arthur won't come down from the
top of the house!" I heard the judge say as
he finished his fish. "Gad! He's behaving
like his ancestress."

He looked about him at the rest of us
while a broad grin creased his jowl on both
sides. I had been exchanging ideas with
Miss Miggs on the subject of Venice, but
the loud tones in which His Honor proclaimed his impression challenged our attention.

"His ancestress!" I repeated blankly, no
one else having volunteered an observation.

"His ancestress!" repeated Judge Miggs,

attacking the game just set in front of him. "She was to have been married from this very house to an officer of Washington's army."

"Odd that I never heard of that."

Mrs. Bowers proffered this observation in her musical tone. She had not shown much interest in the conversation until now.

"The Senator told me the story," proceeded the judge. "The Revolutionary War was raging at that time."

I glanced at the countenance of Mrs. Bowers. A flush which heightened her beauty a moment before had left her cheeks entirely.

"Did the marriage of Arthur's ancestress take place?" she inquired faintly.

"Gad, no!" cried the judge. "Her betrothed came to this very house a day or two before the wedding was to take place——"

He hesitated.

"And the British captured him?" I suggested.

"They captured her," replied the judge with a laugh. "Her lover caught her kissing Lord Howe's aide-de-camp on the top floor."

"Then she married the Briton instead of the Yankee!"

I made the observation as gaily as I could for the sake of lifting the pall which seemed to have dropped upon the subject. My effort was vain, for the retort of the judge seemed to extinguish us completely.

"She married neither," he said shortly. "Until the day of her death she never left the top floor."

I exchanged glances with Miss Miggs. Mrs. Bowers took a sip of vichy. The judge, unaware of the mischief he had done, stuck to the theme all night. He was still pointing the moral of the legend when his car arrived to take him home.

I heard him taking his noisy leave of his

hostess at the door, his loud voice relieved at intervals by a brief remark from his daughter.

II

In the matter of apparitions . . . popular and simple human testimony is of more considerable weight than is the purely scientific testimony.—Mgr. R. H. Benson.

Mrs. Bowers was still very pale when she came back to the dining-room.

"I think I will say good night," she observed faintly.

I saw her clutch the back of a chair. In a moment I was at her side.

"It is nothing," I heard her murmur.

"I am afraid our conversation this evening upset you," I ventured.

But she shook her head.

"Arthur's absence upset me." I could just catch her whisper. "He seemed very much attached to her—once. Now he will not even come down-stairs for a sight of her."

I understood. I could only gaze in silent sympathy into her face. Then she extended her hand, bade me good night, and left the room. I lit a cigar and made my way to the library.

It was close upon midnight as I sank into a great leather chair, yet the thought of bed made me restless. My purpose in coming to this house seemed defeated already. I smoked on in the darkness until I heard a clock behind me chime the hour.

The silver strokes beat the air one after another, until the toll of twelve reminded me that a new day was bringing me a new duty. I got upon my feet with a disconcerting sense that the location of the electric button that switched on the light was a mystery to be solved.

I took a single step toward the window, when a moving something drew my eye to the great bookcase looming in the shadow against an opposite wall. Slowly and steadily the object grew luminous as I watched it.

The wraith of a feminine form defined itself to my staring eyes with a loveliness so appealing that, in spite of the thrill, I felt at the root of each hair on my head I would not have sold the sight before me for a bag of gold.

I saw a pair of sloping shoulders beneath a firmly chiseled neck. I saw a rounded waist and a delicate hand pressed to a smooth cheek. The long robe forming the vestment of this apparition was twined about the curves of the figure after the fashion favored by all sculptors of Greek goddesses. Only the face was kept from me.

I remained for the first few minutes of this experience as motionless as the fantom at which I stared. I did not stir until I saw it glide. The apparition darted and halted, darted and halted, making, it seemed, for the wide door at the extremity of the vast apartment.

As I kept pace with its advance I marveled at the ethereal grace revealed in every stage of this mute progress. The restless clock seemed eager to accompany us through the darkness, so quick was its ticking to my ear.

I had never quivered with so icy a chill as now galvanized my limbs into a kind of movement so like that of the ghost before me that I seemed unearthly to myself.

On, on we went, through the door and out upon the rug beyond. Not until the stairway halted the specter for a moment did it turn. For the first time I looked into the face.

Prepared though I was by the unspeakable perfection of form before me for a loveliness of feature which could alone accompany a presence so angelic, the countenance upon which I was allowed to gaze at last transformed me for the instant into a living statue.

The chin, rounded with a beauty that told

also of strength; the nose, straight, firm,
positive, yet delicate, sensitive, tremulous;
the brow, noble and serene—these details
blended themselves into an expressiveness
that caught its quality from a pair of eyes
into which I could not look. They did not
seem to evade me. The figure kept its gaze
upon the floor.

The light radiated from the eyes was that,
I saw now, which lent its effulgence to the
fantom. I realized by a species of intuition
that one glance of these orbs meant the loss
of consciousness for any upon whom it fell.
No one could have endured the delicious
shock of so much beauty.

I followed to the very top of the next
flight of stairs. The fantom climbed another
story, and on I stole. It made for the gate
that afforded access to the forbidden floor.

There it halted, and turned to beckon me.
I saw the folds of its vesture broaden like a
wide white wing as the moving arm it waved
pointed on and upward. Then it climbed

the stair. I was at the gate, too, now, and I could have leaped the obstacle easily.

An instant recollection of the mother's warning words enabled me to take my eyes from the fantom for the first time. I could not scale the bars of the bronzed gate without becoming guilty of a breach of trust.

Yet I could no more have gazed at all this grace and beauty, fantom and thing of shadow though it was, without slavish obedience to its least behest than Paris and the men on the walls of Troy could contemplate the loveliest of women without falling in homage at her feet.

I put a hand to my brow as I stole guiltily down to the library with all the silence of the ghost I had just beheld. The spacious apartment allotted to me was directly off the library itself. I had but to grope my way to a corner familiar now and find my bed. I fell upon it like a log.

The staring sun roused me with my clothes still on and the vapors of an indescribable intoxication in my head. I made haste to change my clothes. The water of my bath seemed oddly warm, although I took it cold. I was in the dining-room before it occurred to me to look at my watch. It was nearly noon.

An accusing something within me was silenced by the housekeeper's assurance that I was the first member of the household to appear that day at the breakfast table.

"I should like to talk over some matters with Mr. Bowers," I hazarded, gulping some coffee to avoid meeting the eye of this dame.

"Master Arthur will not leave the top floor this day," was her answer, uttered shortly—so shortly, in fact, that I understood from her manner how useless it would be to continue the subject.

"How well you look, Mr. Roegers! Good morning!"

There was no mistaking the tones. The sweet widow was looking in from the garden

through the window, a nosegay in one hand.
I left the table at once.

"I was afraid you might grow fanciful
after that anecdote the judge told us last
night," she began, as I crossed the lawn to
where she stood plucking roses. "Do you
believe in ghosts, Mr. Roegers?"

I gazed keenly into her eyes for a minute.
She was smiling.

"Do I look as if I had seen a ghost?"

I put the question gaily, but I could feel
the beating of my heart.

"There is a ghost in the family, you know,"
she proceeded, following the train of her own
thought rather than the drift of my question.
"It is a sort of heirloom."

I could feel that thrill at the roots of my
hair.

"And what is this ghost like?"

"Oh, I never saw it!"

At that moment my eye caught the glance
of the ancient housekeeper. She was standing at the window. Our eyes met with the

instantaneity of a flash of light and dropped the gaze as quickly. I put another question to Mrs. Bowers:

"The ghost—is it not that of the lady the judge told us of?"

The charming widow shook the masses of her white hair as she inserted a flower above her brow.

"Who knows?"

It was impossible to pursue the topic. I withdrew to the library without even introducing the subject of that interview with Arthur Bowers for which I longed. He did not descend from the forbidden floor.

Until I had taken the measure of this young man, I hesitated to discuss with his mother the delicate themes arising from my brief experience of this unusual household. I had the dining-room to myself that evening. Mrs. Bowers, or so the housekeeper said, was indisposed.

As I seated myself in the library, after a solitary stroll through the shrubbery of the lawn, it occurred to me that, as the authorized biographer of the late General Bowers, I ought to look into his ancestry.

It was an easy matter to find the family genealogy among the volumes on the well-stocked shelves. One county history dealt exclusively with the very mansion in which I was now at work. The edifice was venerable—for America—and, inevitably, had served George Washington as one of his innumerable headquarters.

I was so deeply immersed in my historical reading as to let three full hours slip by. The stroke of twelve had caught me unawares. I thought of the night before and shivered. Then I switched off the light.

The fantom arose from the ground at my very feet!

III

I am entirely convinced of the existence of the spiritual world—that there are real intelligences in that world, and that it is pos-

sible for them under certain circumstances to communicate with this world.—MGR. R. H. BENSON.

Only the fevered ticking of the little clock reached my ear as I stood rigid in the fantom's radiant presence.

There is a famous passage consecrated by Burke to a confession, in his most glorious prose, of his sheer incapacity to describe Marie Antoinette reigning in sovereign beauty over the fascinated court of Versailles.

Homer, too, dared not trust his powers when the beauty of Helen demanded a supreme display of his genius. I can but follow the poet's example in setting down, not an account of the feminine loveliness that now held me as his rapt contemplation of Eve held Adam when first his eye devoured her, but a description of the effect this loveliness had upon my sensibilities.

It seemed, then, as if the whole veil of

woman was rent aside to my dazzled vision from the mere circumstance that I gazed at the fantom. I was myself and not myself—myself in knowing that I was the same man as ever, not myself in feeling weirdly, supernaturally energized.

The incompleteness of my life was extinguished in the full tide of a holier love than mortals have thrilled to. In the inspiring presence of this wraith I felt capable of that faith which moves mountains.

The fleshly and the spiritual ceased to contend as I contemplated with reverence the haunting sweetness before me. I could have conquered the world, founded empires—then. I became the greatest of poets, endowed with a genius breathed into me by this irresistible ghost.

There surged through me all imaginable ecstasies, glorious powers, finer perceptions than ever mortal had. I understood in a flash whatever in my past had baffled me with its mystery. Strains of exquisite music floated through my brain.

How inadequate is the statement that one has seen a ghost! That thought filled my consciousness then like a light streaming from its beacon to the mariner caught in fogs. One does not see a ghost, but surrenders to it as the wax yields to the flame.

I did not come out of this trance until a movement of the fantom intimated subtly to me that I was to emerge from its enchantment. I grew aware that I was following the vision once again through the portal.

The transcendent object of my infatuation conducted me straight to the forbidden floor. I was favored as before with its beauteous gesture. No thought of the ban so recently placed upon my presence here was in my mind, even had I left any power to oppose my mortal will to this immortal spirit.

I followed it unceasingly, unquestioningly. There was no physical obstacle to my progress anywhere. The bronze gate affording access to the forbidden floor had been thrown open.

I set foot boldly upon the lowest step of the stair. The first contact seemed to afford me a definite sensation of personality in the very air. I can liken this feeling only to that bitter blast, that vague uneasiness, which is said to disseminate itself through the night as some vast iceberg skirts the coast of a northern isle. I had caught a chill, and I shivered.

Nor for an instant did I halt. The stairway did not creak. By the time I had set foot upon its summit I was thrilling to some excitation, breathing in impressions like those one derives from moving passages of poetry or strong scenes in a play.

I touched the wall only to find my feelings keener, my sensitiveness to the stimulation increased. All material objects exhaled the mystery stamped upon them by a person or an event in times past of which I was now absorbing impressions. I did not feel that murder had been done here.

The tragedy was all of the heart, of the grief of a soul, of the perpetual and impotent longing of one who, loving, poured out an agony of sorrow to walls that caught the mood. The heart that had been crushed was a woman's. This message, too, I was given by the impregnated air.

The curtain at the summit of the stairway was pushed aside as if by a breath from some other world. I had attained a great quadrangular vestibule, tenantless except for the apparition and myself.

The ghost, preceding me at an interval of some feet, was kneeling beside a wide window through which the warm night air came gently. I beheld a mass of flowers in a vase upon a carved mahogany table. I became conscious of the softness of rugs beneath my feet. I moved as silently as the thing I followed.

No attitude could express the forlornness

of an indomitable grief more appealingly than that of the kneeling fantom. Magnetized by an attraction that made me daring, I touched the shoulder of the ghost.

The whiteness of one arm extended itself to my face. Slowly the vision grew toward me, folding itself closely about my neck and breast until the ghost literally rested in my arms. I could not see the features of my beloved as her unreal lips sought mine.

I could not feel the long tresses I tried to stroke. I spoke no word as I vowed to cherish her in this world and prayed for death that I might be with her in the next.

The tired moon that drooped prettily in the sky had sent a curious beam down here. My eye, habituated more and more to the sweet obscurity, caught now a sharper outline of the vase filled with flowers. The heavy table showed its carved proportions less reservedly.

A mahogany chair, resting as a sleeping monster might rest, upon the floor entered

the enlarging field of my vision.   The impressions made by all these upon my spirits
was one of personality radiating palpably
from them.

Not, indeed, that the objects had themselves this quality.   I mean no more than
that they emitted or effected suggestions of
a personality with which they had been
formerly in intimate contact.   The darkness
of that apartment, pierced by the beams from
the window, seemed laden with such revelations.

The great chair told of one who had reposed, and reposed gracefully, in its arms.
The vase betrayed a secret it had caught con-
cerning her who once delighted in its shape-
liness.

I have always been sensitive to impressions
made after this manner upon things by persons.   I have caught often enough from the
disused furniture of a neglected room veri-
fiable details of the character and life of one
associated with it.   Never was this sense so

receptive in me as at present. But every emanation from the things around me was of evil purport. I was being warned.

"And you will cherish me forever, beloved?"

How I understood that she had put this question I can never tell. The words were not spoken. The language was not earthly. A something within registered the appeal and responded to it. I told of my own unworthiness to be made the object of a celestial passion.

I confessed my longing to reach the confines of the universe in some high quest of a Holy Grail for her sake. I received the outpourings of her passionate regret that in an earthly form years before she had cherished thoughts gross and material, the memory of which left her too sullied for the purity of my faith in her now.

And her fantom arms were wreathed about my neck still, and her bowed head pillowed itself against me, and she quivered with ecstasies of which I partook as a leaf rises and falls with the breezes of a summer's day.

I besought her now to look into my eyes. I saw her head denying that petition. I received some mysterious intimation that the meeting of our gaze must entail an indescribable fatality, not to her but to me.

I conveyed my sense of joy in such a circumstance. Here was the proof of my devotion awaiting her acceptance. Let me but gaze into those eyes and I would wander forever through the universe a blissful spirit. But she only kept her face buried upon my shoulder and held my head with her arms.

I had begun a more impassioned plea when she rushed from my embrace, reeling to the window. I saw her fall upon her knees, cowering. She covered her face with one hand, while, extending the other, she pointed to some object behind me.

I turned and beheld—Arthur Bowers!

There was no mistaking those eyes, that

proud forehead, the delicacy of each refined feature. He was his mother's son. For a terrible moment he and I glared into each other's faces. I saw him raise an arm. He rushed forward. I threw myself between him and the fantom, but when I directed my gaze to its refuge the object of my infatuation had disappeared.

The next moment Arthur Bowers had me by the throat. Then consciousness left me, but not for long. I was prone upon the floor when my senses returned and the arm of Arthur Bowers was about my head.

"I saw her with you!"

He spoke in the musical accents of his own mother, but grief never found utterance so wild. His tone was a revelation. I cried my reply with the voice of a man in panic.

"She made you vows of an eternal love and you pledged yours in return."

He bowed his head once more. I realized the sense of betrayal that tortured him. The ghost had proved unfaithful. I was torn with his own jealousy, but he proved to me that his ordeal had been worse than mine.

"I saw her with you!" he said. "One torture has been spared you. You never saw her when her gaze rested upon—me!"

I hated him for a second of time. Then I conquered my worst self and pitied him. He had removed his arm from my head and was assisting me to my feet.

"We shall never see her again."

It was I who said this. He buried his face in his hands.

"She was too timid," he murmured faintly, "to let us look into her eyes."

The question elicited from me by this remark led to further revelations.

He, too, had held mysterious communion with the infatuating wraith; had confessed a longing to reach the confines of the universe for her sake. To him, too, she had professed regret that in an earthly form years before her thoughts were gross and material.

"It was from love of that fantom, then,"

said I, "that you remained shut up here so much?"

"Yes, yes," was his tragic whisper, "I have been haunted by her presence here by day as well as by night. Your glimpse of her was fleeting. She has haunted me always."

He was forced to bow his head to hide his grief. But in a moment I heard him speak afresh:

"I have seemed to hear her whisper in my ear by day—not once, but always. If your mere sight of her has made you what you seem to me now, what must I be after my long subjection to her spell? You know now why I loathe you!"

We exchanged a glance as he confessed so much. I became suddenly aware of a change in the atmosphere of the forbidden floor. The emanations of personality from things material here had ceased.

The atmosphere was laden no longer with psychical impressions caught from walls and floor. The vase was no more to me now than a work of art. Its mystery had fled.   The great carved table had forfeited its subtle gift of communication.

The terrific emotion which first charged the air with its vibration had been neutralized at last. No visual image of the departed wraith could precipitate itself upon my consciousness in this purged atmosphere again. My mind reverted to the brilliant hypothesis which that explorer of the world of fantasm, Mgr. R. H. Benson, has constructed to fit cases of this kind.

It is conceivable to him that emotions generated by a passed and passing life may be conditioned by the state of mind at dissolution. The living and the dying set up vibrations in "the emotional atmosphere." These continue in agitation.   The place grows haunted.   An appropriate or corresponding vibration can alone break the spell.

"When that meets this," to quote the words of Benson, "the suspended chord is complete and comes to a full close." Or, to

borrow the image of the same high authority,
"an emotional scene which has translated
itself, so to speak, into terms of a material
plane can, like music in a phonograph, re-
translate itself back again."

I felt now that I had the clew to my
ghost.

The lady in seclusion on the forbidden
floor so long ago had been true to her lover
—in her fashion. He had, indeed, surprised her in the arms of another. It was
a sentimental accident in her life.

She had been denied all opportunity to
explain. She was possibly the victim of a
man's sudden impulse. My own infatuation
with the rare and beauteous spirit had led
me far.

In any event the longing of the human
soul to be understood—the craving of this
lady to vindicate herself—persisted while
she lived. It was her most vehement desire
as she passed away.

The very walls, the chair she sat in, the

vase in which she arranged her daily nose-gay, grew sick with this discarded lady's longing.

"If telepathy from living mind to living mind," asks Mgr. Benson, in the course of his study of fantasms, "is a force so mighty as to convey a visual image from France to England, is it not perfectly conceivable that a telepathic force which has been stored, so to speak, in a kind of material battery for years—stored there by the terrific emotional impulse of the original crime—may be powerful enough also to produce a visual image?"

It was so with me.

I did not cease my scrutiny of the countenance of Arthur Bowers as these thoughts ran riot in my head. His mind was too manifestly overwhelmed by the shock it had sustained. He paled slightly and spoke at last in low tones.

"I have nothing to live for."

The words I would have spoken in reply

were cut short by the entry of the old housekeeper. She and I exchanged another such
swift glance as had given me one shock already. Arthur Bowers did not seem to heed.
He merely repeated:

"I have nothing to live for."

"Ah!" I cried, "you forget Miss Miggs."

"True!" he exclaimed. "I had forgotten
Miss Miggs."

Their wedding did, in fact, follow
speedily.

I should note as well that the old housekeeper is no other than that Mrs. Murray,
whose materializations prove so interesting
to students of the occult.

May I add without egotism that my account of the late Senator's career has placed
me, if I may trust the book reviewers,
among the few great biographers of the
age?

The widow was so pleased with the work
that she consented to reward me with the
inestimable gift of herself.

THE FROU-FROU

I had been married exactly nine hours.
As I indulged in fretful whiffs of the cigar and peered through a window at the stars, after returning my watch to my pocket, the inexpressible desolation haunting me from the first moment of Isabel's appearance before the cathedral altar at high noon that day opened a yet lower depth to my sinking spirit. I had arrived with this radiant bride of mine after a long journey by rail at the remote and well-nigh inaccessible shooting box of my uncle, the lieutenant-governor. Isabel, whom the ordeal of a very fashionable wedding in the metropolis, followed by an exhausting ride of several hours in a private car attached to a fast express, had obliged to retire with her maid the moment the automobile negotiated the

mountain roads through the deep forest to the door, was in a bedroom above.

It was a dainty nest to which we had been brought for the first few weeks of a honeymoon, which at one period of our engagement promised—at least to me—to last forever. The perfumed trees murmured even now through the night above the roof of this snug lodge. There was a view of twenty miles from the great windows of the top floor. Outside ran the wide and pillared balcony, about which I had in holiday times played as a boy and to which I now returned, after an absence of years, with the responsibilities of a married man upon my young shoulders.

What positive yet indefinable and baffling influence had established a discord between my Isabel and me? The misery of this problem was profound already, although I had grown aware of the approach of a crisis in our lives only within the few hours since we were made man and wife. The mystery presented itself as one of something lacking in my bride that had been conspicuous in my betrothed. The Isabel I had courted with such ardor was not the Isabel awaiting me above. The difference between the two, sensible and torturing as I had begun to find it, assumed no aspect that I could make precise to myself as I pondered its mystery before the vast fireplace in the hall. There is in personality and in temperament an essence capable of evaporating as subtly as do those chemicals with which the experiments of the laboratory have enriched modern science. That combination of qualities which together made up for me all that went by the name of Isabel had lost one impalpable but precious ingredient that spoiled the sweetness of this hour. This I realized, but more than this I did not know.

The melancholy of my mood had absorbed every shadow of the deepening night outside when I heard the voice of my man James. He conveyed a summons to the presence of my wife. My wife! I said the words with almost the consternation of Othello, for like him, at least just then, I had no wife. I turned from the window and made my way up the wide stairway with the sensation of one contemplating his own introduction to a stranger—a lovely, radiant, gracious, pleasing stranger, but still a stranger. For had I ever loved Isabel, the real, the ultimate Isabel, this trying mood would not be upon me, like a fever.

My heart was beating, hotly beating, as the door of the sitting-room above obeyed my touch. The lamp upon the table shot everywhere its streams of light, but the bride was yet to emerge from an apartment beyond. I closed the door behind me and walked slowly as far as the great length of the room allowed. I halted before a mahogany bookcase, surmounted by vases of ostentatious flowers, set here by the servants in honor of the day's tremendous event.

When Isabel emerged from the seclusion

of the boudoir wherein, with her maid's assistance, she had laid aside the traveling dress, over which so many young ladies were raving hours before, the shadows cast by the lamp but half revealed her presence. I heard only the trembling of a curtain, followed by the light fall of oncoming feet. The first vague sense of revelation came then. A suspicion of the truth, a prophetic intimation of the shock in store for me made even the slightest word of greeting impossible as Isabel advanced. I could but stand there like a man petrified, mutely contemplating the figure of the woman who had risked her future that day for love of me. As she advanced, hesitatingly, even timidly, growing more and more portentous to my straining eye and listening ear in the gleam from the lamp, a realization of the true nature of the catastrophe of my union with Isabel became for the first time complete.

The frou-frou!

This, the invariable, the intoxicating ac-

companiment of her every light movement,
had first lured me to Isabel.   Frou-frou!
The very onomatopoeia of the word, from its
resemblance in sound to the thing signified—
the slight rustling of the skirts of a woman
as she walks—attests the ravishing art with
which the French have reared that monu-
ment of their genius, their own language.
We   forlorn   Anglo-Saxons   must   speak
merely of the rustling of feminine skirts as
a woman passes.   The French have invented
the divine word frou-frou.   Nothing of all
the harmonies it signifies was lacking in the
music of Isabel's least movement when first
her flitting figure lured me to her side.   I
would not imply that she was destitute of
the more tangible charms.   The appeal of
her veiled lids, the waves of her bosom, the
white line of the throat as it balanced delicately the burden of all the beauty above
and below it, suggested to me those broad
lilies between which Narcissus peered to find
his face in the water.   Isabel had fineness of

manner. Isabel's voice was low and sweet. But these things were brought together, as the artists say, they caught an atmosphere from a most characteristic frou-frou.

There was something in the rustle of her skirts when she walked that proclaimed Isabel to me—Isabel! Isabel!—as the blue bells of fairyland heralded Titania advancing amid the flowers of her realm. Isabel affected no gross swish, like the vulgar heaviness of the dowager, kicking silk in front of her with boots a size too small, in corsets laced to suffocation. The lorn nightingale— to steal a phrase from Shelley—mourned not her mate with such melodious pain as Isabel brought me with the whisper of her skirts, the echo of her skirts, the frou, frou-frou, frou-frou! As there is in every poet's line, if he be a perfect poet, the characteristic manner, the individual note, which no cunning of the most servile imitation ever really seizes, so was there in the frou-frou of my Isabel sitting down to dinner or going in to

supper a poetry distinguishable from that of
even the most finely arrayed lady who ever
manifested her shoulders in the most extreme effects.   Her frou-frou was the essence of Isabel, her rare and virginal perfection translated to the ear.

And now, advancing slowly towards me,
adown the length of the vast floor space, the
shaded gleam of the lamp glowing by fits
and starts in her face, Isabel entranced my
ear with no frou-frou!   I strained my listening ear as the starving captive pent up under
ground in a mine must stand rigid at the
first faint sound of the pick that heralds
rescue.   Silence—save for the light fall of
small feet.   I knew now the meaning of the
foreboding that had been mine when nine
hours ago Isabel advanced upon her father's
arm to the altar of the cathedral.   My ear
had missed the greeting and the music of
her movement.   There was a void which all
the organ notes had not sufficed to fill nor
the delighted murmurs of the many wedding

guests. In the thrill of the wondrous hour
set for my wedding I had indeed been conscious of my loss. I had not until now traced
this consciousness to its source.

"Adrian!" She breathed my name lightly,
tenderly, daintily, as she stood before me.
"It is late."

That mocking something in all tragedy
which blends it so cruelly with the absurd,
which renders its most poignant pain more
maddening because it has its origin in the
grotesque, tortured me anew. How in-
formed with the absurd was that pining of
Narcissus at the pool in which he beheld but
the reflection of himself! What could be so
senseless as that weeping of Niobe which
turned her at last into a fountain of her
own tears? And yet the beauty of these
tragedies emerged from the very circumstance that it could persist through the
ridiculous interwoven with all the sublimity.
Narcissus, hailed by the passing stranger
with a query, must have evoked the rude

laugh as he told his spirit's burden. How, then, could I, asked by my radiant Isabel the meaning of my mood, descend to the literal? Frou-frou! It was a mood I had caught from the soul of things feminine evoked by a skirt's echo.

Her arms were about my neck, as I knew they would be. She had rested her head against me, as I anticipated she must. The very actions proved how remorselessly the mere common sense of Isabel must rear its barrier between my feeling then and her interpretation of it. The literal matter-of-factness of this virgin would take note only of the material basis of the frou-frou, missing the symbolism of the sound altogether. She would tell me of that era of transformation between the bouffant hip, entailing petticoats fastened with goodly shirrings to a rather thick band, and the telescoped lingerie of this age of accentuated slenderness. She would tell me how three garments, each with a band plus shirrings at the waist line, aggravated that difficult zone, the curve of the hips. She would tell me that combinations, solving the most profound of all the problems arising from fashion's decree of slenderness for woman, had extinguished the frou-frou. To such details must I condescend were I to undertake with Isabel that crown of love's martyrdoms, an explanation.

And if I, with the man's incapacity to realize the woman's point of view, would never be consoled for the frou-frou by the fineness, the slenderness of Isabel's new lines, how could I expect my bride to grieve over the ecstasy of my lost thrills? The frou-frou is to modern man the poetry of woman. Its extinction marks the loss of an old attitude—that of the trembling, clinging Desdemona. The new woman, clamoring for the vote, asserting her equality with man, proclaiming the gospel of Ellen Key, scorns any such appeal to the strength of a sterner sex as the long reign of the frou-frou consecrated and avowed. The frou-

frou—why, that is Juliet's softness and
Miranda's grace delighting the ear with the
message of man's dominance.   The frou-
frou is gone!   Great Pan is dead!

I understood, now, facing Isabel there in
the moonlight, struggling with the rays
from the shaded lamp yonder, what she had
meant by the hundred and one activities of
her maiden days, the social settlement work,
the study of the newer sociology, the partici-
pation in picketings at strikes.   I had been
pleased to regard these things as phases of
a restlessness that must pass as the years
made us one.   Yet how were we to become
one unless means were found to bring the
frou-frou to my ear again?

"How strangely silent you are, dearest!   I
do not know you to-night."

She had drawn my head down to whisper
the words.   I opened my lips.   I would explain the source of my melancholy.   The
very framing of the petition in my mind revealed to me, by a flash of that illumination

coming to a man with the blinding effect of Saul's vision, that I was bidding the woman step backward along the pathway of time. She was to give up the mode of to-day and revert to the mode of yesterday. Only thus would the frou-frou ever ravish the ear of me. Could Juliet step out of the Verona in which Shakespeare found her to become at once a militant suffragette of our day? Could the militant suffragette transform herself into that miracle of love's slavery, Juliet?

To ask the question was to answer it. I could never thrill to the frou-frou until Isabel had taken what she regarded as a step backward adown the long and painful slope up which her sex had toiled from the time when brides were captured like prehistoric bisons until they went to the altar in dresses relegating the frou-frou to the limbo of the hoop-skirt.

"I must speak to the chauffeur."

This was all I could say in place of the

impassioned plea that would not rise to my
lips.   Before she had proffered a word of
protest, I closed the door between us.   With
all the swiftness of my panic, I raced down
the carpeted stair to where the flicker of the
flame in the fireplace danced in its fantastic
mockeries of my misery and of me.   Light as
my tread had been, the trained ear of my
man James was not taken unawares.   I saw
him standing now before me, respectfully
silent, his shaven face with its summit of gray
hair affording me the consolation of a
familiar thing.

"James!"

I spoke the name with what self-control
I could command.   This man had served my
father in his time.   He understood my most
complex mood.

"Yes, sir!"

It was the respectful and trained readi-
ness of the lackey that found expression in
the tone, but latent was a devotion to me
personally which no gold could have bought.

"I shall leave this place at once!"

"Yes, sir."

The answer was impassive. I knew that behind the tone was the blank amazement that a summons to Elijah's chariot of fire must have brought, but the feeling was concealed like an eavesdropper crouching behind a screen. James permitted himself merely to gaze steadily into my face in the flare of the fire, flickering fitfully as he inquired, in the most respectful manner in the world:

"Will your wife go too, sir?"

I drew a handkerchief from my pocket and passed it over my dry lips.

"No," I replied in a whisper. "We shall go alone, you and I. Have the chauffeur bring up the car."

"Yes, sir."

As the syllables escaped him there reached my ear from a source that seemed remote, in a manner that seemed ghostly, with a faintness like that of a far, far echo, the swift, uncertain whipping of the air which worked upon my heart and brain.

The frou-frou!

There could be no madness upon me, like that of the mandragora with which the Egyptian queen befooled her passion. Only the rustle, the quick, delicate, immaterialized and spritelike race and run of sheer Persian ruffles, or nainsook trimmed with Valenciennes, could have filled the stillness of this night with the beating of such angel wings!

"James! I shall not leave to-night after all!"

The lackey retired with his habitual swiftness and silence. My ear drank in only the rhythm, the cadence, the fairy hum of cambric chafing silk, of sheerest batiste and lace under Chinese satin. The consciousness of all this harmony drawing near and ever nearer was like an ecstasy I had felt as a boy when first I saw a curtain lifted in a theater. I could detect the arrival of the wearer of all these effects at the head of the stairs. I knew when the petticoat fell, fell, fell silkily, from step to step, about its wearer's feet. What can there have been in the weirdness of the spells of Semiramis or of Salome, veiled and gauzed transparently for the dance, comparable with the seductiveness and the subtlety of ruched pleats crushed between a woman's booted feet? Nearer and nearer played the frou-frou through the dark, bringing to my mind the prophet's joy at music in the night.

The spell was broken only by a woman's voice murmuring in my ear. I turned and beheld Isabel's maid. She brought word that her mistress desired my instant presence.

For the first minute or two, coming as I did out of a tranced and raptured condition, I gazed with beating heart into the eyes of the girl before me. She had Isabel's build and dark eyes and slenderness, with an air of shrinking meekness due, no doubt, to a sense of the social position which necessity forced upon her. I made no reply in words. Taking a wallet from my pocket, I pressed into her hand the largest bank note I could find there. She seized the yellowed paper with an eagerness proving how unusual the thrill of possessing a little fortune must be. I noticed now that the dress she wore had once belonged to Isabel, realizing at the same time that the maid must be wearing something else from the despised treasures of the wardrobe of her mistress.

"And your name?"

She stood aside to let me pass first before whispering:

"Lucy, sir."

I gave her a signal to precede me up the stair. The beating of my heart was in tune with the rustle of those skirts as I followed her up through the darkness, lured by the frou-frou, frou-frou, frou-frou!

THE GOLDEN RAT

WHAT secret of her troubled soul could the youthful and lovely wife of old Gerald Lancaster be concealing now from me? She was decidedly the most baffling of all my patients. I was comparatively young, as men in the professions reckon age, yet I had devoted eleven arduous years to the practice of that department of psychology which goes by the name of psycho-analysis. It seemed obvious, from the very first appearance of the lady in my consultation room, that she suffered from the shock of an underlying emotional disturbance. Mrs. Lancaster, that is to say, had passed through a painful experience. She had striven to banish it from her consciousness.

Now what had been the emotional disturbance in her case? I could but conjecture vaguely. Her experience, whatever it had been, was not extinguished. It remained latent in her sub-consciousness, buried below the level of her waking mentality. The case of Mrs. Lancaster was, to use the technical phraseology, one of repression, the experience or emotion which she strove to put out of her mind and her life being what we psychologists call a "complex."

As I concentrated my gaze upon the large but troubled eyes of Mrs. Lancaster, it dawned upon me that the "complex"—the idea or sorrow she strove to annihilate—was emotional, sentimental. Had she formed some unhappy attachment which the fiercest efforts of her will failed to subdue? I made the suggestion which seemed to me the best possible under the circumstances.

"I shall have to hypnotize you."

Speaking in the fluted accents which made her voice harmonize so perfectly with the sweetness of her face, Mrs. Lancaster objected to the very idea. She declined to be hypnotized because she feared the process might undermine the strength of her will. It was not difficult to reassure her on this point. To my surprise, however, I found my patient absolutely unhypnotizable. There remained only the alternative of imploring her to tell me frankly all that was in her mind, all that might be below the level of her consciousness, all that she would hide even from herself.

"I fear," I remarked, as considerately as I could—"I fear you are concealing something from me—something of which you do not perhaps realize the importance or even the nature."

She searched her memory in vain. I had, on the occasion of our last interview in my study, forborne to press her. It was my hope that in the course of a subsequent consultation I should elicit the mysterious cause of her nervous state.

How well I remember that summer afternoon! The wife of old Lancaster had taken her departure, and I stood absorbed in baffling reflections with reference to this most mysterious patient. Slowly, at last, I opened the door that afforded access to the garden stretching from my study window quite to the stables. The garden, like the stables themselves, was a luxury, a whim of mine. The value of improved real estate in my native city made the taxes upon my cultivated acres anything but a trifle. I might have kept a motor car, but my love of horse-flesh made it impossible to give up the stables for a garage.

"More rats, doctor."

It was Boggs, the grim coachman. I found him rubbing down the most spirited of the steeds behind which it pleased me to spin through the streets of the city. Boggs indicated a pail near one of the stalls.

I gazed vacantly at the nestful of tiny young rats. My mind was still absorbed by the repressed "complex" of the puzzling Mrs. Lancaster. I still stared at the seven blind, feeble creatures, too young for even

a growth of hair to be manifest upon their
hides. Boggs had stepped over to my side
by this time. He clutched the nozzle of a
streaming line of hose.

"I'll drown 'em, drat 'em!"

He would have flooded the wriggling nestful in a trice had I not stayed his hand.

"That little fellow there," I remarked—
"he looks different—lighter than the others."

Boggs peered down into the bottom of the
pail.

"Yes, doctor," he conceded, his voice thick
with the disgust and annoyance the sight of
rats in the stables invariably caused him.
"One there is yellow-like."

To the amazement of the honest Boggs, I
plunged my hand among the young rats and
picked up the specimen that had caught my
eye. There he lay now, in the palm of my
hand, blind, weak, helpless. The hairs upon
his odd little frame were sparse. They were
sufficiently thick, none the less, to impart an
aspect of fluffy gold to his coat. I was half

inclined to drop him to his doom among his brothers when his tiny tail waved vaguely. It was covered nearly to the tip with a growth of down that made it look like a golden wand. Before Boggs had closed his mouth from sheer wonder at my behavior, I had slipped the baby rat into a pocket of my coat.

Slowly I retraced my steps across the grass from the stables to the study door. I was in some perplexity. Should I risk an experiment with the tiny thing breathing still in my pocket? The query vexed me as I paced from the desk in my little study to the door of the laboratory beyond. In this laboratory were stored the test tubes, the culture mediums, the beef broth and the apparatus for clarifying and sterilizing through the medium of which I enlarged the range of my biological knowledge•by artificial cultivation of bacteria. Here, too, were the cages in which, at one time, I had bred three generations of white mice. The creatures were all dead long since. I was quite an adept, however, in the care of these rodents. Many a specimen had been inoculated in this laboratory with "cultures" of my own.

Lifting the little rat from my pocket, I laid him, seemingly more dead than alive, in one of my small cages. A spirit lamp had next to be set aflame. With its aid I soon heated enough milk to fill a small bottle, from the corked neck of which protruded a tiny quill. The little rat absorbed the first meal I gave him greedily enough. I had the satisfaction of seeing him curled snugly in sleep upon a litter of scrapped rags before the milk was half consumed.

Many days had not elapsed before I saw the hair upon his coat grow sleek and plentiful. To my surprise, the yellowish tint which had first attracted my attention to the young rat deepened into one of fine gold before I possessed him a week. In a fortnight he was strong enough to climb the side of the box which was his home in my laboratory. He ran about the floor so recklessly that I was forced to keep a careful lookout for stray cats and dogs. My original fear that he would prefer the freedom of the open air or of the cellarage to my laboratory proved groundless. He seemed to be destitute of the quality of timidity. Never in my experience of pets had I acquired one so recklessly tame. It was a source of perennial delight to him to spring from my shoe to the hem of my trousers and climb up to my shoulder. There he remained perched contentedly while I read or wrote or even walked about. As day succeeded day, the exquisite golden color of his coat grew richer. I discovered his tastes in edibles, especially for roasted chestnuts, and gratified it to the full. He seemed to tire of bread and milk as he grew fatter and more golden of hue. I fed him upon cake and nuts. His place of refuge, when pressed for one, was the pocket of my coat. Again and again have I felt him stirring about there while I rival of a patient. The rat—he was a good-sized animal now—took refuge in my pocket the instant old Pawkins was announced. Pawkins, I should explain, was one of the prominent bankers of the city, who had long been under my care because of his neurasthenia. It had not been easy for me in the beginning to trace the source of his disorder. It seemed due primarily to an idea implanted in his mind by the physician who first treated his symptoms. Pawkins had been told that he was threatened with Bright's disease. He had seized this diagnosis eagerly. His ailment was, on its physical side, solely due to a false suggestion. Unfortunately, however, I found it no easy matter to win my way to his confidence. There was in his mind, latent and unconquerable, a suppressed "complex," an idea he would not avow, a thought that held him prisoner. No effort of mine could bring it to the surface. In accordance with my practice, I did not force the revelation I sought from old Pawkins.

I was content to bide my time, as I was biding my time with the wife of Lancaster.

The elderly financier had barely seated himself in a chair facing me when I got a sudden fright. It seemed as if he had brought a dog with him. I thought of Philander in my pocket and had difficulty in suppressing an impulse of alarm. A closer inspection of the crouching figure at the feet of old Pawkins sufficed to correct my blunder. It was no dog that sat so near him. It was rather a shadowy outline than a reality, a suggestion of a shape. As I gazed the thing seemed to be a wolf—or shall I say the wraith of a wolf? A minute or two elapsed before I could withdraw my gaze from what I felt now must be a spectre. I had seen what was too evidently a ghost, for when I dropped my eyes once more to the floor the thing had disappeared.

It was easy enough to get rid of old Pawkins after a few perfunctory questions. When he had taken his departure, I gave myself up to a profound reverie. Philander had emerged from his retreat and was gorging himself on the floor with roasted chestnuts. It was borne in upon me at this moment, for the first time, that some connection must exist between the golden rat and a series of emotional and physical experiences and sensations in myself. I asked myself if the golden rat had not communicated to me the symptoms of that fevered state in which I now so often found myself. The state was one of exhilaration—like the first effects of some delightful stimulant. It was an exhilaration which wore away. It left, unlike the thrills that go with opium, no baneful consequences. It brought me a singular capacity to verify with my own eye —at intervals—the fact that practically all sources of illumination emit an ultra-violet light playing no part in ordinary vision. This is the result of the circumstance that the eye is sensitive only to a small proportion of the radiation reaching it. There were

times, however, when my eyes became more
than ever camera-like, detecting and measur-
ing the intensity of what physicists call the
infrared rays. I could see at such times by
the aid of a light which physicists have pronounced invisible or at least discernible only
through photography.

It occurred to me, after the departure of
old Pawkins, that the wolf I had seen at his
feet was an optical eccentricity in me. I
recalled just then a fit of trembling in
Philander while he lay concealed in my
pocket. I recalled, too, the peculiarities of
his conduct when certain other patients were
in my study. The golden rat was subject to
an inexplicable panic whenever the wife of
a certain clergyman poured the tale of her
neurosis into my ear. Philander took refuge
under a bookcase or in the remotest recesses
of a drawer in my desk. My eye chanced
to light upon his frolicking form as I
pondered these things. He held a walnut
in his forepaws and, perched upon his hind

limbs like an educated poodle, was devouring the morsel greedily. I waited until he had satisfied his appetite and then called him by his name. In a trice he was upon my shoulder.

The exigencies of a laboratory experiment that day required the use of a pair of black silk gloves. These were in my lap. The rat was creeping around my neck as I drew one of these gloves over my left hand, fitting it snugly and carefully from force of habit, although my mind was engaged solely with the mystery of the Pawkins wolf. On a sudden I saw a minute speck moving against the blackness of the glove. It was a mere mite of a speck, but it shone in golden luster as it flitted and fluttered.

The darting and dancing mite in the palm of my gloved hand was a flea.

A flood of light was let into every nook and cranny of my mind the moment I had caught the golden insect on the tip of my finger with the aid of a dab of vaseline.

Philander, then, was infested with fleas. They were like himself in their peculiarly golden aspect. I brought the rat from his place of rest on my shoulder down to my knee. The critical inspection of his fur to which I abandoned myself—not neglecting a microscope in the process—revealed a quantity of golden fleas. I was unable to identify the species. It is true that the varieties of flea already classified are infinite. I had studied a few in my student days. Here was a species as new as it was strange. There could be no doubt that the fleas on Philander had been the agents of the spread of some infection to me. My symptoms of late had been very puzzling.

I was quite certain that Philander could not have imparted to me the bacillus of any infection so dire as plague. That dread disease appears only in fleas which have bitten affected rats or persons at least twelve hours prior to death. The organism causing the disease itself must exist for a certain interval in the body of Philander, there to undergo a definite alteration, before it could induce an infection in me by transmission through the flea. And there was no known case of plague affecting a human being sufficiently near to involve Philander in the slightest suspicion.

The dilemma of my situation seemed greater on the following morning. I found my fever slightly higher, although the exhilaration was quite pleasant. I observed an accentuation of the eccentricity of my vision. I detected ultra-violet light without the aid of an instrument. There was one close friend to whom I could turn in this crisis. Having ascertained over the telephone that Thorburn, the renowned specialist, who had been my classmate at the medical school, could receive me at once, I hastened to his office.

My brilliant friend, whose researches in microbiology fill the world with his fame, had a touch or two of gray at the temples, I the thought that would not leave him, the longing he had put out of his mind. His wish for a child to bless his union with Florella had been put from the upper level of his consciousness into that lower level of forgetfulness where his "repressed complex" lay buried. All men living, I knew, bore in their minds the wishes, the aspirations, they had buried in the well of the subconsciousness. Not until this moment did I suspect that the longing buried in the mind, the fond wish one dare not avow but over which one gloated inwardly, was a wraith, a ghost. Thorburn's buried wish was haunting him. The stork at his side was its ghost.

Not a word of all this escaped me; no hint of the presence of the grave bird passed my lips. I laid my case before him to the extent of avowing my fear of some infection. He examined me from head to foot. He made every laboratory test possible in the circumstances. As he came and went, now peering into my eyes, again holding a tube

aloft in the bright electric light of his laboratory, I saw the stork follow him, sit at his
feet, flap noiseless wings or prepare for
some wild flight that was never even at-
tempted.

"There is no organic disorder," was Thorburn's report at last. "I see no evidence yet
of the presence of any infection. I can let
you known definitely in a week."

The stork, invisible to Thorburn, eyed me
gravely as I took my leave. In much perplexity I walked slowly to my home, letting
myself in with my own key and repairing
to my study with a profound problem on my
mind. The first thing was to find Philander.
He had a trick of fashioning a nest for himself out of old newspapers under a corner of
my desk. I called him by name. There was
no response. At first I suspected him of
hiding from me by design, a thing he was
very prone to when he feared being shut up
in his cage for the night. He had a great
affection for the chimney. The soot in that

retreat begrimed his coat most sadly, although he never failed to wash himself clean the moment he emerged. There had been no fire in my study since the spring. I thrust my head into the empty grate and called his name loudly. There was again no response.

I was not in any great alarm. He had a way of disappearing now and then, sometimes for as long as twenty-four hours. My one dread was that a stray cat or dog might pounce upon my pet. There was now nothing for it but to compose myself in my easy chair and ponder the events of this day.

My eye wandered vacantly over the papers and test tubes forming a litter in front of me until a gleam of something like light, a flash like the twinkle of a distant star, enchained my glance. The shimmer and flash were a series of stains upon a handkerchief. I picked up the silken article in some bewilderment at first. It looked like some fantastic flag with suns in gold designed upon its center. My own initials

worked in a corner of the piece of silk
brought back to my recollection a slight
bleeding of the nose which had troubled me
that morning. I had applied this silk handkerchief to my face. The slight hemorrhage
ceased. I had given the matter no further
thought. Now I saw spots of shining gold
where in the morning my blood had stained
this piece of silk a bright red.

In my bewilderment I took the handkerchief over to the window. There could be
no doubt now of the brightness of the gold.
Never in my experience had I heard of man
or woman who bled gold. I resolved to
despatch the handkerchief to Thorburn for
an immediate analysis. The ringing of the
bell, a voice at the door and the entrance of
a visitor postponed the execution of this
purpose.

"And how is our rising young psycho-
analyst?" cried a cheery voice, as a burly
form broke rather than appeared through the
door. "Upon my word, that last talk of

yours upon the mental mechanism of the banished idea has made you famous."

My visitor carried with him, I saw now, a late number of the official organ of a psychological society. One of my studies was given a very prominent place in the periodical. I glanced at the printed page and then rose to greet old Graham. I dearly loved this man, for he had been one of my most honored preceptors in my student days.

"My dear Graham!" I cried.

A silvery dove fluttered about his head, but I was accustomed by this time to my capacity for this species of visualization and I betrayed by neither word nor glance the effect of the sight upon me. The dove, I could see, corresponded to the system of ideas making up the "complex" of this good and generous man. What a contrast to the predatory old Pawkins, whose repressed ideas emerged in spite of himself under the guise of a wolf—at least to my vision! It

has been well said that in the psychical
sphere complexes have an action resembling
that of energy in the physical sphere. A
system of ideas may lie latent in a man's
mind for a long time, becoming active only
when stimulated. This explained, no doubt,
why the dove hovering over old Doctor Graham flitted out of sight now and then.

"My boy," said the old man, looking somewhat anxiously about him before he sank
into the chair I brought, "are we alone?"

I nodded. There was an anxiety on his
mind which became more manifest as he proceeded:

"You may have heard that one or two
well-defined cases of plague came recently
to the notice of the board."

I recalled such a report. I had first heard
of the matter at a gathering of physicians
some time before. Graham, who was in the
service of the Board of Health, had taken
the matter seriously at the time, but the
affair had dropped out of my thoughts long

since. The old man leaned forward to impress me with what he had now to say:

"The cases have been increasing. We have made up our minds to make war on the rats."

"The rats!"

I spoke in a tone of some consternation. The words brought the missing Philander back to my memory.

"The rats," repeated Graham solemnly. "We have actually discovered the bacillus in the bodies of no less than three rats."

"Were they rats caught in the city?"

"In this very neighborhood. We have been quietly trapping here and there. We don't want to start a plague panic until we are sure of our facts."

I watched the dove flitting above his head and I thought of Philander. Had they trapped the golden rat? I had to steady my voice with an effort before I could put my question:

"These rats—they are the ordinary gray variety?"

The elderly physician looked troubled.

"Yes—and no," said he slowly. "Our traps have contained gray rats as a rule. But in two instances we have captured a very peculiar variety of the animal—gray rats with a spot of gold on the breast."

He drew from his pocket as he spoke a small leather casket. It opened at the touch of a spring. I saw the stuffed skin of a gray rat, splashed in the spot indicated with gleaming gold.

"This rat," explained old Graham, lifting the stuffed object up for my inspection, "was trapped in the house next door. It is one of six marked in this very extraordinary manner—a species never seen before by any authority I have consulted."

I took the stuffed rat from the grasp of my elderly friend and examined its aspect critically. Those who have never studied at first hand the habits of a rodent of such sinister fame can form no idea of the natural cleanliness of the little animal. Apart from the tendency of the flea to infest the rat, it is one of the daintiest of quadrupeds, not, indeed, without a beauty of its own. The spot of gold between the forepaws of this specimen set off its gray coat effectively.

"Although we have trapped rats all over the city," proceeded old Graham earnestly, "they are all of the usual gray type except those few caught next door. I have just been setting traps in your cellar."

The thought of Philander made my blood run cold at these words. I gazed in blank dismay at the physician. What had become of the golden rat?

"Have you"—I faltered before I could speak the question completely—"caught anything here?"

"My dear lad, the traps have just been set—two of them. I can let you know the result in a few days."

"You spoke just now," I resumed, in as natural a voice as I could command, "of having isolated the bacillus in the blood of some of your rats. How about these?"

Graham took the stuffed rat from me and looked it over.

"We have isolated a most curious organism in the blood stream of this little creature," he observed. "A golden microbe."

"What disease does it cause?"

I tried again to speak naturally, but I remembered the golden blood I had shed and felt faint. What if I had acquired a new and strange leprosy from the bite of the golden fleas of Philander!

"Strange as it must seem," I now heard Graham aver, "the microbe—it is really a bacillus with its nucleus and protoplasm—gives rise to no discoverable disease in the rat infected by it. Perhaps it is responsible for the gold spot."

He touched the flaming breast of the stuffed creature.

"The remarkable thing," the old doctor added, "is the golden element in the rod-like process of these organisms. One might almost say the blood of this rat was golden."

My mind reverted to the analysis of my own blood cells which Thorburn was at that moment engaged upon.

"You don't mean to say," I rejoined, smiling, "that you have discovered a form of bacteria that is beneficial to the invaded organism?"

"I'll know more about that when I have trapped more of these rats," the old man told me. "I expect to get some here by the end of the week."

The moment he had taken his leave, which he did almost immediately, the dove fluttering out with him, I rang up Thorburn.

"Come over at once, if you can," he said at the other end of the wire. "I have news for you."

I put on my hat and paced the streets hurriedly. I caught sight of a policeman at the corner taking a prisoner to the lockup. The man in the toils of the law was obviously a beggar. At his heels trotted a snow-white lamb. The policeman was followed by a hawk. I turned and gazed after the pair until both had disappeared around a corner. Was I doomed to see at the heels of every fellow creature the symbol of his suppressed idea, the ghost of his complex? I fairly raced to Thorburn's door.

"There is something very remarkable here," was his first utterance, as he led the way to his laboratory. "What do you make of that?"

He held up a glass slide of the sort used in experimental biology. It was stained with a golden spot.

"Your blood," said he. "It has yielded a pure gold bacterium of the strangest character. Your blood is like the stream in which King Midas bathed—filled with golden sands."

He had scarcely said the words when a

movement of flapping wings behind him
drew my eyes to the stork. It stood for
a moment erect and then retreated to the
remotest corner of the laboratory, where it
regarded both of us with all its characteristic solemnity. Thorburn was unaware of
the ghostly presence. He sat me down in a
great chair and questioned me most minutely
regarding my symptoms.

"You must have contracted a disease of
some sort," was his final verdict.

"Fatal?"

"I am using the word in a technical
sense," he laughed, seeing my sober visage.
"Disease is, in one aspect, the invasion of
one organism by another. Your organism
has been invaded by a new and strange
bacterium, all gold. You say it does not
debilitate you?"

"I never felt better in my life."

I glanced unshrinkingly into his puzzled
face. I had carefully concealed from him
the fact that I had acquired the novel faculty

fresh form among the bacteria? Has not
Burbank evolved new forms of vegetable
life by a seeming miracle of metamorphosis?
But this was by no means all that Thorburn
meant. May it not be that the bacteria
which cause disease are prejudicial only because they represent types of degeneracy?
They have been corrupted, that is to say, by
passing in and out of the blood streams of
a fallen human race. It is we who have
poisoned the bacteria, not the bacteria which
have poisoned us. In that event, science is
on the wrong track. We must purify our-
selves, in order that the microbe may regain
its pristine purity and become the blessing
it may have been to our prehistoric ancestors.

I remained in a profound reverie long
after Thorburn had finished his elucidation.
If what he told me was true, I had acquired
an infection, but it was a benevolent process,
a source of strength. The flea had trans-
ferred to me from the body of Philander an
organism that endowed me with a more won-

derful power than had been possessed before by any mortal man.

"By the way," remarked Thorburn, suddenly changing the subject, "shall you be
at Mrs. Lancaster's dance to-morrow night?"

I started at mention of that name. It
had been weeks since I had given a thought
to my patient. I replied vaguely that I expected to dine at her house. My mind was
running on Philander once more, and I bade
him adieu with some abruptness.

There was not the least trace of the presence of the golden rat when I arrived breath-
less once more in my study. I called him
by name more than once. In vain. I
thought of the trap set by old Graham. Before visiting the cellars I resolved to peer
up the fire-place.

"Philander!" I called. "Philander!"
There was a faint sound up the chimney. In
a trice I had thrust my arm up the sooty
embrasure. Philander descended, clinging
to the sleeve of my coat. What a begrimed

and blackened aspect his body now wore! I
set him upon my desk, where he fell to an
assiduous licking and washing of his fur. I
had the satisfaction of seeing him restored
to his original color before he had completed
his toilet. Then he frisked his way to my
shoulder, upon which he perched with all
his familiar sauciness.

It was vitally important to keep Philander
out of reach of the trap set for him. I might
have ordered the stableman to remove the
horrid instrument, to be sure. Yet that
might inspire too much wonder in the mind
of old Graham. On the other hand, I must
not let the golden rat out of my sight. He
spent the night securely locked in his cage.
He was not released during the entire next
day. His squeaks of protest were incessant.
I would have no mercy on him.

After some reflection, I resolved to attend
the dinner and dance at the house of Mrs.
Lancaster. It seemed the surest method of
providing for the safety of Philander. It

would be no difficult thing to take him with me, concealed in the pocket of my coat. The golden rat was always shy when strangers were about. I knew that nothing could lure him from the refuge my clothes afforded him if there seemed the least prospect that he might be handled by an unfamiliar acquaintance.

The hour appointed for the dinner at the house of Mrs. Lancaster was already chiming when I entered the dining-room. The guests were barely a dozen. I was already familiar with their faces. Philander was snugly ensconced in a breast pocket of my dress coat. He was fast asleep.

"What a stranger you are, doctor!"

The words were uttered by my fair hostess. I had never seen a more pensive melancholy upon her exquisite features. She sat at some distance from me at the foot of the table. I made my very best bow and smiled before I sat down to the oysters.

"Ha!" exclaimed Thorburn, who chanced

to be seated directly opposite me. "You are
looking very well—still."

There was a meaning smile upon his
kindly features, and I was at no loss to
interpret it. The silent stork at his side
peered myopically into my face and flapped
a pair of wings. I saw the hideous wolf
peering greedily from beneath the chair of
old Pawkins, who absorbed champagne
moodily. Old Lancaster had a fierce ferret
on his shoulder, a circumstance to which I
was inclined to attribute the restlessness of
Philander, who stirred now and then in his
sleep. The most interesting object at the
dinner table to me was a hyena, which
chafed and fretted at the back of a distinguished member of the judiciary. One
old lady, whom I had met before, and who
was a notorious gamblei, revealed to my
secret vision as her repressed complex a
gigantic pike. The fish literally swam in the
air over the dame's head, darting every now
and then ferociously at prey invisible to me.

"I hear," observed Pawkins at last, "that there is a case of plague in quarantine."

The wolf leered over his shoulder and licked its hideous jaw. The introduction of so dire a theme at that crisis in my life spoiled the dinner for me. I listened to the flow of talk about me, hearing much speculation regarding such things as fleas and the bacilli. Mrs. Lancaster seemed only half aware of what was transpiring around her. My attention was drawn particularly to her by the suggestion of a wraith upon her shoulder. I had looked eagerly in her direction more than once, hoping to descry the symbolized embodiment of her complex. That there was a form of some description outlined upon her shoulder seemed clear. I thought at first it might be a bird. Later it wore the aspect of a fish. At last, I had to abandon the effort to define to myself the shadowy thing moving from her right arm around her shoulders to her left. The secret of my patient's repressed complex was almost mine. Again and again it eluded me. The vexation of that circumstance made the end of the dinner a welcome relief. I strolled into the smoking room, listening vaguely to the din of the violins, tuning for the dance.

Finding myself alone, I peered into my pocket. Philander was fast asleep. I hated to disturb the repose of the golden creature, and for that reason remained with my cigar alone to the last possible minute. In the end I was obliged to make my appearance in the ballroom.

There was not a dancer on the whole vast floor without his or her attendant creature. A member of the United States Senate was closely followed in the mazes of a waltz by an opossum, while his partner, a lady with some fame as a landscape painter, kept a porcupine in her train. The pastor of a church led a vampire in its flight among the dancers, above whom it poised itself, fanning sundry individuals with its

wings. There was one gigantic crocodile
in a corner which every now and then
abandoned the shelter of the wall to cavort
and caper after the founder of fifteen
hospitals. In short, wherever I looked
I beheld specimens of a zoology unsuspected by those who danced in and about
among pelicans, pumas, guinea pigs and
polar bears. One gigantic creature, symbolizing the repressed complex of the most
famous lawyer in the country, was evidently
an antediluvian monster. It appeared to
my astonished gaze somewhat like a lepido-
siren. These creatures were like the men
and women they all haunted in turning,
twisting and waltzing to the music. Now
and then there were collisions of a signifi-
cant sort. I beheld a fierce fight between
two bantam roosters, one being the repressed
complex of a well known novelist and the
other that of a successful merchant. The
repressed complex of the merchant's wife—
a lily white hen—watched the struggle com-

placently. When the bird symbolizing her husband was routed from the field, I saw the lady begin a fresh dance with the novelist.

It occurred to me to seek my hostess. She had not appeared on the floor for some time. I felt an uneasy movement in the pocket of my coat. For the sake of Philander rather than to secure any repose for myself, I sought the shelter of the Japanese room. I was quite alone when I sank back wearily upon a sofa and looked at my watch. It would soon be time to go.

I was opening my cigarette case when Mrs. Lancaster appeared in the doorway. Her exquisite features wore an unusual gravity, even for her, as she advanced. I divined that she had a revelation to make. Whatever I might have said remained unspoken, however, in the shock of discovering a golden rat perched upon her shoulder. For a moment the idea entered my head that Philander must have escaped from my pocket. I perceived, as soon as I had looked at the creature again, that I could not implicate Philander. The golden rat on the shoulder of Mrs. Lancaster was smaller than my pet. It was of less robust physique, softer in outline, more graceful.

I had placed my hand in Mrs. Lancaster's outstretched fingers, when a flashing form sprang from the pocket of my coat. There was a tiny shriek of joy. I saw Philander capering and shrieking on the floor with the diminutive creature that followed him from the shoulders of the lady who had so long been my most baffling patient.

"I think," I managed to say, my eyes riveted upon the gamboling creatures on the floor — "I think I have the key to your case."

I saw a flush spread from her cheek to her brow. She bowed her head and, still holding my hand, sank upon the chair from which I had just risen. It seems odd to me, as I look back upon all this, that I never suspected the mutual infatuation out of which our repressed complexes were built up. She loved me. I saw the avowal in the eyes she turned up to my face as I bent over her. As our lips met, I felt a convulsive shudder at my breast. I put my hand in my coat. There lay Philander.

To my profound amazement, the rat bit me. With an effort, I repressed an exclamation of pain. Thrusting the little creature, who seemed disposed to escape, back into my pocket, I literally fled the place.

There was no one stirring as I entered my dark study and turned on the light. How long I sat absorbed in my reflections I knew not. There was a patch of crimson in the sky when at last I got up from my desk and walked over to the window.

How long had this woman loved me? Through what circumstance had it become possible for her to identify me with the golden rat? I was, evidently, her repressed complex. As I stood at the window pondering these things, a figure moved across the lawn.

"Boggs!" I called.

It was that honest hostler. He had just set about the business of the stables.

"Have you seen Mrs. Lancaster?"

"She was here to see you last month, sir."

"Why was I not told?"

"Why, sir, I thought the girl would tell you. She waited for you here an hour. She saw the golden rat."

"You mean," I interrupted, "that you showed it to her."

"I told her how fond of it you had grown, sir."

Here then was the explanation I sought. The mention of the golden rat reminded me at once of Philander. I had quite forgotten, in the bewilderment resulting from my experience with Mrs. Lancaster, to shut him up for the night in his cage.

"Philander!"

I called him again and again without effect.

"Boggs," I remarked, "do you remember when Doctor Graham was here to set his traps?"

The stableman scratched his head with a most aggravating stupidity. Yes, he remembered the visit of the physician. He recalled the setting of the traps. He had not seen them placed. He did not know where they were. I lost no time in getting to the stables with a lantern. The search was fruitless. There were no traps that I could discover. Boggs remembered that the old doctor had talked of the cellar. Thither we repaired. I found no traps. The failure to discover the devices did not console me in the least. I knew the old doctor to be a cunning and experienced rat catcher. He might have hidden his deadly devices under a loose plank or in a remote closet.

The full dawn of that morning brought

no Philander. I ransacked the house without avail. Neither trap nor rat resulted.
The day following was but a repetition of
the disappointment. I discovered to my
dismay that Doctor Graham had left the
city for a few days. The official of the
Board of Health to whom I telephoned
offered to send an inspector to my house at
once. The doctor had left at headquarters
a list of every domicile in which a trap was
set. I closed with the offer immediately.
The result was another vain search of my
premises.

The despair to which I was reduced by
the continued disappearance of Philander
led me to overlook, at the time, a curious
circumstance connected with Thorburn. I
saw him for a brief interval on the street.
He was not accompanied by the ghostly
stork. The detail made no impression upon
my mind for an hour or more after I had
parted from him. Then I hurried to the
street. A week before, I would have beheld

the repressed complex of any passerby. Now I saw dozens of pedestrians. No beast or bird attended any.

Turning back into the house with a strange giddiness in my head, I was halted by the arrival before my door of a motor car. Out stepped old Graham.

"The trap!" I shouted. "Where did you set it?"

I observed that no dove fluttered about him now.

"The trap?" he echoed. "In your study, of course."

I staggered after him. He led the way to a corner of a bookcase into which I had not once dreamed of peering. With loud triumph, the old doctor lifted a trap on high. It held Philander, cold and dead.

"Very, very remarkable," he observed. "Wouldn't you say this rat has a golden color?"

His face reflected a grave anxiety. I spoke up savagely:

"It's a golden rat. Are you afraid of it—it is dead."

"I hear you've been looking for me," he said, wiping his eyes with a handkerchief. "I was called out of town by the case of Mrs. Lancaster."

"Is she ill?"

He lifted the dead form of Philander from the trap before replying:

"Her people had her committed to a sanitarium. She insists that she is followed everywhere by a golden rat."